ELWOOD REID

WHAT SALMON KNOW

Elwood Reid is the author of the novel *If I Don't Six*. He is a regular contributor of both fiction and nonfiction for *GQ* magazine, and has been a carpenter, a bouncer, a cook, a bartender, and a writing instructor. He lives in Brooklyn, New York.

ALSO BY ELWOOD REID

If I Don't Six

WHAT SALMON KNOW

ANCHOR BOOKS

A DIVISION OF RANDOM HOUSE, INC.

NEW YORK

WHAT SALMON KNOW

stories by ELWOOD REID

FIRST ANCHOR BOOKS EDITION, SEPTEMBER 2000

 Published in the United States by Anchor Books, a division of Random House, Inc., New York, and simultaneously in Canada by Random House of Canada Limited, Toronto. Originally published in hardcover in the United States by Doubleday, a division of Random House, Inc., New York, in 1999.

The following stories have been previously published:

"What Salmon Know" in *GQ* (February 1997)
"Happy Jack" in *GQ* (October 1998)
A slightly different version of "Buffalo" appeared in *Ploughshares*, Vol. 25 / 2n3

The Library of Congress has cataloged the Doubleday edition as follows:

What salmon know: stories / by Elwood Reid.—1st ed.
p. cm.
1. United States—Social life and customs—20th century—Fiction. 2. Working class—United States—Fiction. 3. Men—United States—Fiction. I. Title.
PS3568.E47637W47 1999
813′.54—dc21 98-55516
CIP

Anchor ISBN: 0-385-49122-0

Author photograph © Nina Egner Moore
Book design by Dana Leigh Treglia

www.anchorbooks.com

Printed in the United States of America
10 9 8 7 6 5 4 3 2 1

for NINA AND SOPHIA

CONTENTS

WHAT SALMON KNOW

OVERTIME

Drew looks down into his coffee, hands shaking. They've got the screws to him. He'll have to ask someone to keep their press running and that means overtime. Nobody at the plant wants it anymore. Not even Jim Dandy, who used to eat up the hours because he was saving to buy one of those tricked-out Dodge pickups with the Cummins diesel. He's got it and now there's one less go-getter at Drew's disposal.

Fuck asking, Drew thinks. He'll just tell somebody they have to work a few more hours. He gets paid to pull the strings on the zombies, that's how one of the suits in the upper office describes the job. All day long Drew walks around seeing strings hanging from people.

He scans the press chart. Names, then numbers. Sometimes he forgets the names and when he sees them in the hall he says, How you doing—press ten, right?

Settles on Flo Levine, press #16. Flo's due, by his figures, straight forty-hour weeks since January. If not Flo, then Frank Cooper—good solid family man. Reads the Bible at lunch, keeps his press clean. One of them has to say yes. He decides to ask Flo first, then Frank.

There's a knock at his door and Renfield from the office waves a redsheet at Drew.

Know about this? Renfield says, pointing at the sheet and the numbers.

Drew smiles. Nods.

Taking care of it?

Again he nods. The office loves to show him redsheets when production's fallen off mark. Red means correct at all costs. Red means he's not doing his job, not pulling the strings on the zombies.

Overtime, Drew says.

Never hurt anybody, Renfield says. How much?

Drew holds up his fingers. Just a pinch.

Renfield winces and scribbles this down in his little notebook. Later he'll punch this info into his computer. The computer will spit out an Hours vs. Product chart, worker efficiency numbers, etc.

After Renfield has made his way back to the office Drew jots down Flo's and Frank's names on an old bill of lading. Looks at his watch.

He makes his way onto the plant floor. Machines hum and crack like some mechanical storm. God, he thinks, how did I end up here after all of that college? Then he thinks about his paycheck. He's young. There are thirty people under him and only ten above him. He feels good about things, but not too good; there's that extra five pounds he'd like to lose before Christmas, a mole on his right thigh that's been changing colors lately, and his wife, who's been after him about spending more time together, which is difficult because she has her own career selling educational packages to schools, not to mention aerobics class, the book discussion group *(Crime and Punishment, Lord Jim)* and her sick mother.

They want children. Mostly her, but he's willing to go along. It's time and all that. Her clock, she says, is ticking. But he can't think of those things now. He's promised himself to only concentrate on work when he's inside the plant. Start thinking about wife and then kids not yet born and the day drags.

Now, he has to think about getting the product covered and making it jive with his hourly allotment versus production. It means overtime, and overtime has become a dirty word in the plant after the half-day on Saturday was added last summer. It means bye-bye weekend.

He could wait and ask somebody on Saturday to stay the extra hours, but if he's learned anything it's get the hours on Friday, that way they still have Saturday night to do whatever it is the zombies do with their weekends—bowl, barbecue, rent movies, sleep, drink, rake leaves, look at catalogues, fight with wife or husband.

No, Drew thinks, better to spring it on Frank or Flo right now. Butter them up, make them feel special, wanted, needed and all that.

Still, he feels as if he's dipping into somebody else's life, redirecting it for a few hours here and there. Not such a bad thing, he thinks, and better Frank Cooper or Flo than one of the old-timers, who seem to complain about everything and who every year seem to be moving slower and slower, falling off their daily quotas. They've got pensionitis and he can't blame them. Twenty-five years pushing a button would kill him. Wonders how they do it. Like maybe they shut their brains off, go to sleep and wake up older, half deaf with a two-pack-a-day habit and varicose veins from all the standing, but with a pension. Then what? Buy a Winnebago, enjoy the grandkids? But then what's he working for? What's at the end of his tunnel? Happiness? Kids? A train's beam?

Flo sees Drew coming and starts shaking her head, steps off her press platform.

Oh, no, she says.

He smiles and wags a finger at her. He's always liked Flo. Quick with a dirty joke. Hard worker with family to feed ever since her husband took off for Texas with a waitress named Mindy. Maybe not even half bad to look at when she was younger and before the factory went to work on her complexion.

Hours, Flo? Drew says. He has to shout. Watches her pull product out of the machine and toss it into the creeper cart next to her platform.

Flo flips him off and laughs.

Ask somebody else, she says. Unless you want to babysit

my kids for me. It pays five bucks an hour. How much you make here, Mister Clean White Shirt and Tie?

Are you threatening me? Drew asks. He can't help but smile.

Just stating the facts is all, she says.

You're lucky I'm a nice guy, he says.

Nice guys finish last, she says.

She laughs some more and Drew tells himself that he's a pushover. He should have just ordered her to work, but Flo's got a few tricks with men and he doesn't mind.

Okay, okay, he says to Flo. I give, I'll ask somebody else.

Thank you, hon, she says. You're a sweetie pie.

He finds Frank Cooper's press and watches him work for a minute. Metal in one end, product out the other. Drew doesn't know a thing about the machines, only the people behind them and how to manage their hours. Frank Cooper's no slacker. A company man through and through, who can see his way to the pension. Drew taps him on the shoulder after he's fished out the last gasket clamp.

Frank, he says. I need you to work a double—you can do that, can't you? It's just we're a pinch behind and, well, to be honest with you, Big Joe will hear about you offering to work the double, and not that it matters, it's just . . . quite frankly it'll make him happy and you'll be doing us a favor. A big-time favor.

The air brakes give on the press and the top spindle does a half-turn to gear down. Drew flinches, understands how these things snip fingers and mangle hands.

Frank's face drops. He puts a gloved hand to his temples and tugs at his eyes. Fluorescent lights flicker.

Not tonight, Drew, he says. My daughter's got a volleyball game. It's her first start and, well, I was going to watch her play and take her out for pizza after with the wife. Sort of a family night, you know.

For a minute Drew thinks about the possibility of asking Frank to stay late on Saturday. But that would be worse. And what if they don't catch up? Maybe a press goes down tomorrow and they fall even further behind, then what?

So he gives Frank the eyes—a little stare to tell him that he's the boss, that he can, if he wants, make Frank Cooper's life a little bit miserable.

Aw come on, Drew says. I thought I could count on you.

Frank grinds his jaw, good blue-collar work ethic ripping his guts up.

You'd be doing us a big one, Drew says. I mean, I've asked the others and nobody wants the work.

A big lie. Only Flo. And she pushed him right over. But there are the numbers. Numbers never lie. Eight more hours at forty whatchamacallits an hour ought to catch them up nicely and make the truck in the morning. The fact is, Big Joe probably doesn't even know Frank Cooper from John Doe, even though he signs the paychecks each week and walks the plant when the mood takes him. But he's busy with that new girlfriend of his, the one with the plastic face and store-bought tan. Not to mention his golf game, the boat on Lake Erie, fund-raisers. So who's Frank Cooper to Big Joe? A big nobody, Drew figures. A little overtime. But six or eight more hours to Frank Cooper is part of his life, especially when there's family involved. And Joe's not doing the asking, he's paying Drew to pull the strings, see to it that his business makes good on its orders.

He watches Frank's face. Presses whine and grind. The air smells like oil and degreaser, some cigarette smoke floated on top.

I guess I could make a call. Arrange for my wife to go. I don't really want to but . . . , Frank says.

Drew watches Frank's face change colors, light gray to red gray as he agrees—kisses his daughter's game good-bye.

That's just great! Drew says, pumping his arms in the air like a coach. I'll get Herman over here to reset your press and then we'll be rolling. Why don't you take a break while that happens. Coffee?

He looks at Frank, the wrinkles, bad skin, gray hair, face shaped like a kidney, and he thinks how strange it is for somebody as young as he is to be telling Frank what to do. He smiles some more and pats the man on the shoulder. His shoulders are soft, like bruised fruit or fallen bread dough.

Next time, Frank says, next time I won't be able—I'll be busy or something. I'll say no.

Drew ignores him.

That's just great, Frank. Boy do we appreciate this.

He notices how Frank's got pictures of his family hung up around the work stand. Wife, two daughters. Drew bets it's the oldest daughter who's got the game. In the picture she's tall, dirty-blonde hair, smile full of braces. The other daughter, short and pudgy. Neither of them look a thing like Frank.

On the way back to his office Drew checks his watch and calculates how many minutes left until the shift kill whistle blasts through the plant. After that he can go home, while Frank stays and takes his bacon out of the fire, because as the upper office sees it, this shortage, or miscalculation as they call it, reflects on him.

When he first started he'd stay with his operators when they had to put in the overtime. Tell them jokes, ask them questions about their families and make like he was their friend because he felt bad. But that got old and nobody noticed anymore. Just another salaried fool blowing his off hours trying to assuage his guilt or kiss up to a boss who wouldn't know kissing-up if it fell on his head and crushed his skull. So he quit being the good soldier and instead took off with the kill whistle and went home to his wife, lawn mowing, dinner out, the occasional movie, while his operators picked up the extra hours for him.

So he waits ten minutes. Stares at the clock. Thinks about the wife. Five minutes.

Taps his watch.

Kill whistle.

Air brakes whine and stomp all over the plant. Work-booted feet trudge down the aisle and line up in front of the time clock and it's the weekend for a couple of hours.

Next morning he checks the time cards and sees the overtime on Frank's card, feels guilty, but Saturday's are half-shifts and everybody's in a good mood because the office staff is out. Anything goes now. Drew plays the radio over the intercom, rock 'n' roll—whatever. There are donuts in the lunchroom, guys stumbling to their presses still drunk from the night before.

He flips through the cards again and notices that Frank hasn't punched in today. He didn't mean for Frank to work the overtime and take Saturday off. This will put them behind next week and he can't have that. Can't ask for any more overtime, doesn't want Renfield knocking politely on his door with more redsheets and his nice suit, telling Drew what the computer says.

He decides to wait a few minutes, then go out and ask around the plant. It's quiet, nobody comes by his office to ask for aspirin, tell dirty jokes, or kid him about sitting on his ass pushing paper around a desk all day.

He thinks about the sex he and his wife, Diane, had the night previous. The way her hips looked when he slid her underpants off. The smell of her skin. Again she told him how they should try for a child, how it would make things better for the two of them. She wants a girl.

He has another bad cup of coffee—not enough grounds and the water at the plant is poisoned. Then he strolls out onto the factory floor. The machines drown out the music and he wonders what the big deal is about having it over the intercom when nobody can hear it.

He goes by Frank Cooper's press. Empty. Sam Murkowski punches the kill switch, steps off the platform, removes his gloves and walks up to Drew.

Did you hear? he says.

Sam's eyes are red, his cheeks webbed with broken blood vessels. Everybody knows he's a drinker and that he sometimes fills his thermos with beer or vodka and lemonade. He never misses, though, so Drew can look the other way when he smells it on his breath.

He gets up in Drew's face. Did you hear what you did, you sonofabitch?

Sam makes a fist and bites his knuckles then points to

Frank's press. It's empty. Just pictures of his family and the girl, the one who plays volleyball. Drew wonders if they won and if she spiked the ball, because she's tall for her age. Up to her daddy's shoulders. And a pretty girl.

Herman the mechanic steps into the aisle with a hammer and wrench in his hands. He's not wearing his dentures because it's Saturday and there are no secretaries to impress.

No. I can't hear you, Drew says.

And he can't. The presses buzz in his ear. Sam leans into him.

My God, he sobs. They found her last night after the game.

Who? Drew asks.

Frank's daughter. They found her late last night. Down by the lake, behind the school. Dead. Missing first. They saw her leave the locker room and that was it. She got swept up.

Drew folds his arms. He doesn't understand. Two more presses brake down and then kill out. He can't help it but he starts thinking of how this is going to put him behind. Can't have people taking breaks and shutting their presses down when the mood strikes them.

Then Betty Brownlow walks over, earplugs hang from her neck, swing against her fat breasts. Larry Gelp comes too and Drew's reminded of a scene from *Night of the Living Dead.*

Come again, Drew says.

Sam blinks, stares at Betty and wipes his face with a thick forearm.

Damn you to hell, Betty says. She's dead. They found her down by the lake with a phone cord around her neck.

Didn't you hear? Everybody says you knew this morning. Horrible. A terrible thing. You can't imagine.

Who? Drew asks. But then it hits him and he knows—the girl in the picture—Frank's girl is dead.

Drew backs out of the circle and they point at him.

Jesus, he says. When? Where?

It's all he can manage. He feels cold asking, but his lips are moving. He's talking. He has to know when.

Frank was supposed to go to the game and then take her out afterward. Drive her home, Sam says, waving his fist at Drew like he wants to hit him.

But his wife? Drew asks. Only he doesn't want to know any more. He feels sick. Frank's wife was supposed to make the game. He remembers Frank telling him that yesterday. He's sure of it and he holds on to this fact like a drowning man. Then he starts thinking about Flo and how easy he let her off. How she should have been the one to stay and not Frank.

She's dead and you let it happen. She never came home and Frank's wife never went to the game. Sick with the flu. The girl was supposed to get a ride home from one of her teammates, Sam says.

No, Drew says, this can't be.

Then he thinks perhaps this is some joke—they've played them on him before. He looks at them. Waits for one of them to crack a smile. Nothing.

He looks at Larry Gelp and Larry just shrugs.

You did this, Sam says. You made him work overtime. He should've been there and none of this would've happened.

Drew puts a hand to his face. For some reason he thinks of Diane at work.

What's her name? Drew asks.

Stephanie, one of them yells.

They stare at him and wait for him to say something. Instead he walks away.

Later, on his way home, he stops and buys the paper and looks for mention of the crime. Surely front-page stuff in this not so big town. Only there's no mention. Sports scores, a headline or two about Bosnia and California. He checks the high school scores and sees that the local high school won their volleyball game. For some reason it makes him feel better. He sees S. Cooper under the server scores—three points. Good, he thinks. There are other names with larger numbers after them, but here it is in the paper. S. Cooper with three points. Numbers, he thinks, I'm good at looking at numbers. He cries and turns up the radio so loud his windows vibrate.

Then he drives home to tell his wife.

After he's told Diane and the following day's paper has run a large front-page piece on Stephanie Cooper, and a picture of Frank holding his wife, Drew gets up the nerve to go back to work. Nobody talks to him. Big Joe has given Frank an indefinite leave before jetting off to Puerto Rico with his new girlfriend.

A coffee tin stuffed with tens and twenties sits in the lunchroom. The same tin they use for group Lotto and when George Miller lost his hand on #13 trying to pull a loose bolt out of his press. Now somebody has written

Frank's name in blue marker on an old time card and taped it to the side of the tin. Drew walks by and empties his wallet into the coffee tin. Nobody sees him and he thinks it's at least fifty dollars. He wishes he had more and that somebody would see him donating.

Drew hides in his office and makes only one call up to Stan Larson, who covered for him on Monday. Stan tells him it's no big deal and hangs up. Drew hides until just before lunch. He sees Herman in the hallway and Herman looks the other way.

The lunchroom is quiet. Nobody plays radios or talks. Instead they whisper and Drew hears his name slither out of cupped hands. People point and stare.

He goes home early and watches television all night until he's sure Diane is asleep. He does this for ten days.

At work he lets the numbers fall off and is afraid to ask anybody to work over. Betty glares at him when she passes him in the hall. Even the space cases avoid speaking to him.

He makes it through another month before Big Joe sends down one of those inner-office memos informing Drew that he's being replaced in two weeks because he's missed too many days. Accounts are behind. Production is off.

Drew's thankful for the note, he was never much for face-to-face with Big Joe, and besides, nobody talks to him. They blame him for Frank Cooper's loss.

He'll find another job, he thinks as he walks out of the factory for the last time, cardboard box under his arms with his personal effects. Nobody says good-bye or shakes his hands and he's glad—doesn't want to see the factory ever again and there's a moment in the parking lot, just before he's about to climb into his car, that he promises himself to never take a job that involves bossing people around. A girl died for him to find this out about himself? he thinks. He went to college for this?

Three months later the paper runs a big story on how they've caught Stephanie Cooper's murderer. His name is John Bruno and he worked with her in a pizza parlor where she bussed tables part-time on weekends. There is a picture of him in a sidebar. He's older and worked in the kitchen and was obsessed with her, asked her out on dates. Confessed to everything. How he waited in his van after the game and grabbed her just out of the school's back door and how he took her down to the lake and wrapped a cord around her neck. He says he feels no remorse. The arresting officer calls him a monster. Several other people, former neighbors and one ex-girlfriend, say they are shocked, that he was a quiet young man and seemed nice enough.

Drew reads the article to his wife over breakfast while she does her leg raises in the living room. The coffee machine spits and pops on the counter. There is toast in the toaster oven. Dirty dishes in the sink and he hasn't shaved for three days.

They got the bastard, he says, pointing at the article.

It's over then. Poor Frank Cooper, she says. Then continues counting. Fifteen, sixteen, seventeen, eighteen . . .

I can't believe it, Drew says. Somebody called in an anonymous tip.

Twenty, twenty-one, twenty-two . . .

Frank Cooper will return to work, Drew reads. He says he can go on with his life now, that he won't ever forget what this man did to his family. Says he wants him to pay.

Poor man, Diane says. Frank Cooper, I mean. Let me see the picture again.

Drew flinches, stares at the paper, the picture of John Bruno and the Coopers. In the picture they're crying. He wonders what kind of tears they are. Relief? Mourning? Surely not joy.

Twenty-eight, twenty-nine, thirty . . . Done, his wife says. She comes over to the table and puts a hand on his shoulder. She smells like sweat, her hands are wet and warm. Drew notices a thin line of perspiration on her upper lip and remembers a time when he found this sexy. A time when she wanted children.

Today's the day, Drew says. I'm gonna find a job. I mean, this is just the sort of news to get me going. A real kick in the ass.

Diane hugs him. Since the murder things have been bad around the house. She can't tell him that it's not his fault—he won't listen. They've stopped trying to get pregnant. In fact he hardly touches her anymore. She has to touch him, and when she does, he stiffens. Everything is different. His life has been divided into before the murder and after the murder.

They don't talk about when he's going to get it together. It's worse when they do, like something has died between them and their lives are on hold because of it. Instead she goes off to work and stays late, aerobics, book discussion group, sick mother. Comes home to find him on the couch or in the bedroom. She circles promising want ads in the newspaper. Leaves him notes on the fridge listing places he might send his résumé. So when he says today's the day some little hope lights its fire in her.

Yes, she says. Today's a good day. A fresh start. You'll look for something good. A job you can be happy with. Not some musty factory job where you wear the same tie and pants every day, but a real job with a future. It'll be good and I can ease off a bit at the office. Not work so much. Take some time and things can get back to normal.

Yes, Drew says. I want that.

Part of him wants to open up the paper and read the article again. Look at the black-and-white photos of Bruno and Frank Cooper. But he doesn't and Diane keeps talking. She's happy. Sunlight tips through the windows, breaks across the table. Drew sticks his foot into one of the bars of light to put a shadow in it.

She says, Because they found him, and, well, Frank's going back to work. He's trying . . . so maybe you should because after all it wasn't really your fault. Just bad timing is all. It might have happened sooner or later . . . I mean to say he was after her and the fact that Frank could or couldn't come to her game might not have made a difference. These types—what's his name?

John Bruno, Drew says.

They lock on to things—get ideas. This Bruno, he wasn't going to stop now, was he? He wanted her—had to have her.

Drew nods. He wants her to stop but she doesn't.

Monsters like Bruno don't ever forget. They're relentless, is that the right word? Driven by their urges and you couldn't have helped it. You were doing your job. How could you have known?

She stops, wipes her forehead with a towel and pours herself some juice. He goes to the fridge and pulls out a can of beer. It tastes like aluminum, but he drinks it all down. She looks at him. Says nothing about how early it is. If he needs a beer, well then he needs a beer.

He smiles at her.

I mean it, he says. I'm going to try. Really I am.

She nods and starts toward the shower.

He catches a frown on her face. Looks down at the beer in his hand as she comes back out of the bedroom with nothing on. He barely notices what her body looks like and she starts to say something to him. Tears in her eyes. She wants to tell him he's broken her. Can't take living with a stranger, this man living in the after.

Good-bye, she says. He nods and goes back to the paper and hears the shower go on.

He can't stop thinking about this Bruno guy and he tries to remember all of the times he's had pizza at the pizza parlor where they worked. Once? Twice? He wonders if Bruno ever touched any of his food. Sliced some pepperoni on his pizza or grated the cheese. It would fit, he thinks. The coincidence scares him. Then he thinks how it's possible he saw Frank's daughter bussing tables. But he can't remember.

On her way out the door Diane kisses him lightly on the cheek, takes the empty beer can from him, rinses it in the sink.

He does not go out—gets as far as the shower and then

stops. Instead he stays in all day, starts watching television, hoping there will be something on about the arrest. He keeps telling himself that he should put on one of his suits and go out looking for work, maybe go have copies of his résumé made—make Diane happy, show her he's trying. Make an effort. But the day slips away and when she comes home he's still on the couch and she doesn't say a word to him, just goes into the bedroom and closes the door.

Later, after Bruno's trial and after Diane has left him, moved out to an apartment next to the shopping mall, Drew starts looking for a job again. He tries to call her but she won't take his calls. He's gained weight and he knows that he looks strange, face puffy, circles under his eyes. He drives by her complex, his car full of empty Styrofoam coffee cups, candy wrappers and newspapers folded open to the want ads. He remembers some statistic about how few people find jobs in the paper and then he begins to notice how many guys there are like him, out on the streets, looking for work, slightly out of shape, losing their hair.

He looks at his reflection in the rearview mirror and realizes that this waiting outside her complex is creepy and that it might scare her if she were to come home and see his car, their old car, parked in front of her new apartment. So he leaves and stops calling her and after a year he gets the divorce papers in the mail and signs them.

She gets the house and he moves into a double-wide next to a landfill. His street—a loop, really—is called Pine Court. There are no trees, just shrubs and crabgrass and people sitting in lawn chairs next to gas grills. He hangs a bird feeder outside his window and watches the cardinals and jays crack sunflower seeds and fight for spots on the perch.

John Bruno gets life and at his sentencing he asks to speak. I finished something, didn't I, he says, and for that I am not sorry. You take care of the ones you love. I put her away.

Frank Cooper lunges out of his seat to stop the monster from talking.

The newspaper runs a picture of Frank Cooper lunging, mad as hell. And then there is nothing more. The papers move on to other stories and by this time Drew has a job, managing a small office for a direct mail company. No overtime or telling anybody what to do. The secretaries and mail boy know their jobs. The salespeople ignore him. He fills his days with paperwork. Makes sure the copy machines run and have paper. After work he goes down to Delaney's Sunset Bar. Orders a hamburger or fish sandwich for dinner. Beers and then a shot of whiskey to sleep on. The bartender's name is Riley and he knows all about Drew's divorce, his shitty job and the murder. He's heard a thousand stories and Drew's story is no better or worse than the others. As long as Drew tips, Riley will pretend to listen, give him a napkin with his drink and put the ball game on if he wants.

After work on a Monday, Drew stops off at Delaney's to celebrate the second anniversary of his divorce from Diane. He tells Riley this and Riley just nods, pulls a shell of beer, sets it in front of Drew.

Thanks, Drew says.

Rough one? Riley asks. The day, I mean. Besides the divorce?

Better give me a well whiskey, Drew says. He thinks about calling Diane, maybe apologizing to her, but she's already remarried and pregnant.

He tells Riley this too.

Fuck it, Riley says. Water under the bridge. Life goes on and all that good shit.

Drew sighs, knocks back the whiskey and points a finger at his glass. Riley refills, waits for his tip and then goes back to his bottle sorting and sink full of dirty glasses.

Drew stares at his glass. Tastes the whiskey and thinks about work in the morning. He can hear the clang and rattle of dishes in the kitchen, the hum of the dishwasher. If he closes his eyes he can smell the grease and even see the machines, the presses he never understood and the people behind them punching buttons, making things happen, the time clock and dirty factory floor.

He finishes his whiskey and points at Riley for another. Promises himself that he won't close his eyes and see the machines in his head. A man next to him stares and for a moment Riley thinks he sees strings hanging out of the man's shirt cuffs, big gray dangling things like cords or veins.

He blinks and they are gone. The man is just a kid with nothing up his sleeve, no work or hard times behind him.

Riley refills.

A waitress cracks her gum and stands impatiently at her service station. She looks right through Drew and then he looks around the bar and knows why—the bar is full of guys like him, hiding out in rumpled suits, drinking, trying to get somebody to talk to them. He turns away, puts the whiskey to his lips and closes his eyes. The machines come into his head again. He tells himself that it's only a dishwasher, maybe a meat slicer he hears and that the factory was a long time ago—that he was a different person then. He went to college, got a job, married, maybe even loved, lost, had his life divided. And now what? Hours to push through. Work and water to put under some bridge?

He drinks until the whiskey is all gone, the glass empty.

He wants more.

LIME

The first thing the old gal does is have me check on a dead horse. Been dead a long time. The sun's had its way with it. The horse or what's left of it now is covered with maggots and beetles that move in waves over the bloated hide.

I've never seen so much ugly in one place.

"Ate some nightshade," she says.

"Not too much horse sense," I say.

"That's why they live on farms," she says. She's rich and got all of the answers.

She says her name is Mrs. Johnson, but I know this already. I tell her mine is Maynard, which is neither here nor there. Right now I'm passing myself off as a farmhand. My résumé—hands like T-bone steaks, broad back and short, fat legs good for pushing wheelbarrows and bucking hay bales onto flat carts.

Before this I worked deck net and line on a boat up in Alaska after flunking out of Ross Technical College. Spent every sea-rolling day, cold and wet, beating salmon to death with a nailed bat. Had myself figured for some real money until we lost a man overboard running nets a day past the season's close.

Left the ghost ship. Wandered over to Valdez and earned enough money shoveling snow off of roofs for a ferry ticket back to the lower forty-eight. Uncle Fran put me up on the floor of his trailer and let me take meals with him when there was extra. When he wasn't out looking for work we hung around the Loft watching sitcoms and ball games, cadging dollar drafts and playing cribbage.

Uncle Fran's one of those end-of-his-rope types—body used up, mind numb and gnawed. No more salad days for him. "Look at me," he says. "LEARN!" Only when he's drunk it sounds like EARN.

Either way I nod.

So Mrs. Johnson is my new hope. I know she'd love nothing more if I was to call her Miz Johnson and flinch when she speaks. All this land and nobody to work it is the word down at the Loft. I know all about her. Figure I can get a room, maybe a meal or two, seven dollars an hour.

I make her for a hard woman.

"Got a Ford 1500 on the farm somewhere?" I ask.

I can see the gears cranking in her head. She has flat cheeks, short unwashed hair and eyes like a banker. Packs a punch in riding pants, but she's a little past her prime, so I put away the pussy-hound bit.

"Last hand we had rolled it down the pond embankment," she says.

I know the pond, full of bigmouth bass and a water slide for her son who has oatmeal for brains and has to wear neon water wings when he splashes around in the shallows chasing tadpoles and water beetles. I know this from all of my sneaking and creeping—job research.

So when the ad ran in *The Northeast Breeze* calling for a farmhand up at the Johnson farm, I was pumped, primed and ready to go. I even know that her husband does nothing for a living, except read bank statements and wire money around.

"I was thinking maybe we could drag it back in the woods some and let the worms and stink beetles do the rest," I say.

A clot of flies comes off the carcass, and Mrs. Johnson holds her ground and grits her teeth.

"My son tried to pull the eyeballs out yesterday for good luck," she says. I watch something quit in her face and I try my best not to laugh.

"Is that so?" I ask.

She goes into the whole story on how her oldest son Warren's been wrong in the head since birth. Only she gets fancy, calls him "special." Says he likes to play with dead things and goes crazy for rock music. Then she tells me how they've rigged up speakers around the farm so that Warren can play at being a deejay. "It makes him happy," she says. Just then Warren's voice crackles over some speakers in the distance. Mrs. Johnson frowns, marks time with her boots on the grass, and we stand, dead horse between, farm around, all hot and green, as her boy's voice gives the weather report. SUNNY, HOT, WARM, BRIGHT, MAYBE SOME RAIN FLOWERS . . . SHOWERS TAPING OFF TOMORROW.

Mrs. Johnson shakes her head.

The whole Warren thing breaks her heart twice a day. Not to mention the weather reports. I know about her other offspring; the daughters in colleges out East, the youngest son growing his hair long and trying like hell to give up on the family fortune.

But there's the dead horse and it's some kind of test. Like, how bad do I want a job? Bad enough to get knee deep in smelly death?

"I'll take care of it," I say.

I slap my hands together and rub them in front of her face so she can see the calluses.

That just about seals the deal.

"It pays eight an hour, plus the guest house," she says, "after six months, we'll put you on salary."

I know that once I'm off the clock, they'll have me doing all of the extras, like running errands or playing pal-buddy with Warren. I can already hear Uncle Fran ranting about how salary is the working man's cancer. "Work hourly, motherfucker," he says.

But a job's a job and I let out a real beamer and shake my head.

"I got references if you like," I say. "Been to Alaska and it damn near broke me." I show her my hands again. "Worked like a dog."

Flies that have been all over the blown and swollen parts of the horse land on her face, alight on her lips, and like a hard woman, she don't move.

"You got the job," she says. "Do it any way you want. I just don't wanna smell it. Can't have the kiddies thinking something died, now can we?"

On the way to the guest house Mrs. Johnson rattles off the duties. She's got a million. The acres of grass that need mowing make my ears buzz, my back ache. I could grow old keeping this farm green and level. Bushes to trim, roses to wrap in the winter, twelve horses and a handful of ponies, a dog named Dirty Bill who walks with a limp and needs to be fed twice a day. In the winter, there is snow to shovel, icicles to consider, hay to knock and salt, and still more horseshit waiting for me every morning without fail.

Inside the guest house, a green-shuttered affair with primrose and hock holly crowding its oak-shaded planks, Mrs. Johnson shuffles around nervously. I catch sight of myself in the mirror.

I look like hired help.

"I expect you to keep the place looking square and neat," she says, handing me a worn leather notebook with my list of chores and responsibilities in it. "My husband thought it would be a good idea to have the whole farm written down." Her face sours, cheeks pinch. Five gets you ten Mrs. Johnson can't stand the sight of her husband's pale body.

She screws her eyes at me. I smile again and this seems to relax her. She gives me a minute to flip through the notebook. "Two hundred acres, a pond, horses, three pastures and enough grass to choke all the cattle in Texas," she says.

I say, "Just me?"

"There's the cleaning lady, Darcy. Marcia's the groom. You'll meet her. She works with the horses and will let you know when something's not getting done. And then there's you . . ."

"Maynard," I remind her.

She writes this down on the back of a crumpled IGA receipt. I know she'll be checking on me. This is a small town. She'll hear reports of a bar fight or two. Maybe some dirt on Uncle Fran, how he's a welfare loaf, spent time in County.

"We understand each other?" she asks.

I nod.

"You'll be a busy man," she says.

I catch her eyeballing the nicotine stains on my knuckles, entertaining burning-drapery fantasies, smoldering hay, horses spooked by smoke, trapped by flaming beams.

I try licking my knuckles, but the stains are there to stay.

"Do you smoke?"

"I quit." This is a complete bare naked lie.

She don't bite, just gives me the old General Patton up-and-down stare.

"I'll get started on that horse," I say. On the way to the barn I toss my cigarettes in the trash and flip off good old RJR Nabisco. For eight dollars an hour I'd drink Mrs. Johnson's bathwater.

A couple of hours later and that bathwater don't look so

good. In fact it looks like a whole lot of dead horse, which gets me thinking how shovel work is for suckers and convicts.

A blister the size of a silver dollar appears in the middle of my palm. It cracks and weeps and I have to wave my hands around when I'm not digging to keep the flies from drinking off the blisters. After a while they bleed.

Mr. Johnson drives up the dirt path in his BMW with the windows rolled down, to check on me. I take stock of him—pale fish-belly face, small girlie-man hands, and glasses pushed too far back on his nose, which magnifies his nervous, pervert-looking eyes. I can see he's afraid to get out of his car, so I wish some of the flies on him, but they're too busy having a time with me and the dead horse.

"Ahh, yes, the new man," he says with this bullshit British accent.

I grunt at him.

"Nice work, now isn't it?"

"Just about got it buried," I say.

The wind shifts and blows a whiff of dead stink at him. He covers his face, shoots me a quick wave and drives off. It's all I ever want to see of the mister. The horse goes whoosh and plop when I roll it into the hole. Its belly splits open and half the insect world pours out. I shovel like a sonofabitch.

Warren follows me around a lot, watching me work and sweat keeping his folk's place neat and green. Mrs. Johnson talks to him like he's a child, even though he's as tall as I am, strong in all sorts of wrong ways, pale just like the father and scared straight of mother.

I tell him lies about Alaska to keep him busy.

I am in love with the groom, Marcia. It's on account of how she combs her hair with a horsetail brush when she thinks nobody's looking. That and long hours on the riding mower equals wicked fantasies—Marcia in the hay, Marcia flashing me her tits, etc.

Darcy, the cleaning lady, hates my guts because I tracked peat moss in the main house rescuing some water-starved ming trees from the den. I don't consider this much of a loss, because she's sour in that special middle-aged, failed-at-everything lady way.

The Johnsons are ghosts on the place—shadows in tinted windows, voices on the intercom.

I don't sleep nights because they've got the barn wired right into my house so that I can hear the horses breathe and shit. They tell me it's for vandals and barn fires, and how I'm responsible.

Mrs. Johnson has referred to me twice as a caretaker.

I keep telling myself that it's just a job—another load of crap to quit when I get sick of it all.

On Sundays I sneak Uncle Fran onto the place. We watch ball games on my television and drink sixers until our palms are wrinkled and white from can sweat. The speakers wired into the barn get him going. He looks at me and says, "What in San Hell are you gonna do when they come to wire you up, boy?"

I toss him another beer. Tell him it's on me. Then I show him the book of chores and he weeps. Uncle Fran's a jealous bastard.

A week later I'm eating breakfast to Radio Warren. Today is his birthday. Thirty-one years old. He plays himself birthday songs and talks about his cake and party. The caterers have been setting up since sunup. Tiki torches, fake palms, and plastic clamshells strung across the yard. They've even brought in sand. Mrs. Johnson tells me I'm to help pick up after, but to stay out of the way during. I go to my stalls.

Always shit to clean. Job insurance.

After the stalls, I help Marcia clean water bowls. It's only nine and she's already sweating and I want to lean out over her hair and smell her, look down her shirt and all that. I got her figured for late twenties, maybe some college, because I catch her reading philosophy books during her lunch break. She calls me "you" and "hey," but I don't mind. Once I caught her looking at my arms as I loaded straw into Snoopy's stall. I filed this away as evidence—likes muscle.

"What do you do at night?" I ask her.

"I had you pegged for a lot of questions," she says. "Just another nosy man." She runs her cracked nails along the rim of a bowl, dried saliva flakes off. She hits the bowl with water. Watching the water flow through her hands is about my limit. I'm a sucker for a nice set of hands.

"Read," she says. "Sometimes I go to the movies in town."

She tries to send me packing after the water bowls, but I stand and watch her rub Super-Orange into Ramlight's mane as he stomps and chortles. She shoots the hose at me. I've seen her do the same to Dirty Bill, the farm dog, who don't do much else except lay around licking himself, all day. I go down to the toolshed and saddle up the weed whip.

Warren finds me laying waste to sumac and milkweed. I'm covered with plant blood, dirt and sweat. Warren is in his swimming getup, too long striped shorts, arm preservers. He points to his back where a Red Devil spoon dangles. I click off the weed whip and take stock.

Two of the three hooks are in good and deep. He is scared and bleeding. A trail of what looks like thirty-pound test trails behind him like a veil. "Sonofabitch," I say.

Milkweed seed floats between us and for a moment I want to follow them off this farm before the salary noose comes for neck.

"I got fished," he says, doing his level best to hold back the tears. "It hurts. Oh, boy does it hurt."

I push the lure and his face, which always seems to have the wrong emotion floating across it, curls into what I'll call a smile with a little scream offstage.

"Who did this to you?" I ask.

"It's my birthday," he says, smiling, crying.

"Happy birthday," I say. "Now come clean, Warren."

But it's no use. He sits in the dirt and cries some more.

This one's for Mother, I think.

I take him back up to the house. Mother Johnson goes into a rage. Warren starts crying again and I feel like hurting somebody. Mrs. Johnson doesn't like my cut-and-nip plan for getting the hooks out. So she takes him to the hospital instead.

"Suit yourself," I say.

Mrs. Johnson glowers and off they go.

I'm back at the weed-whipping when the Warren caravan pulls in. Warren waves at me and has his mom honk the horn. Ten minutes later he gets on his speakers and tells the whole farm about his wound. He gets through half of "You Light Up My Life" before jerking needle across vinyl and repeating the story again. He even screams a few times for effect.

"I hurt," he says. "I hurt deep down."

Back to Debby Boone from the top.

Then Mrs. Johnson calls me on the intercoms to the main house.

At the house Darcy scowls at me. I can already see her cooking up some scheme which implicates me in the treble-hooking of Warren. So I knock a little dirt on her clean floor, and toss in a few scuff marks for good measure—small stuff.

Over the speakers Warren announces he has stitches. Then he spins a little Tony Orlando and Dawn.

Mrs. Johnson receives me in the foyer. She smells like a hospital. Mr. Johnson is nowhere to be seen and I like it like that. The air-conditioning makes my teeth ache. She tells how she suspects kids fishing for bass in the pond. Pegs them for picking on Warren.

"Had to be," she says. "He didn't go and stick himself with that lure."

"What do you want me to do?" I ask. I can feel the salary beating between us.

"I want you to stake out the pond," she says. "That pond is Warren's swimming hole. I can't have the town punks sneaking in fishing. This is, after all, private property."

"I'll get right on it," I say.

Just then Warren flaps into the room chewing at his plastic hospital ID bracelet and pulls up his shirt to show me the needlepoint.

"Looks real good, Warren," I tell him. "In Alaska they put grizzly spit on cuts."

"Really?" Warren asks.

"Maynard here was just leaving," Mrs. Johnson snipes.

Warren's face goes blank as he pads back into the cool of the house. Suddenly I want to be back out in the barn watching Marcia finish off the last of her chores.

On my way out I catch a squint of Darcy frosting a cake shaped like a radio. Upstairs on Radio Warren, Tony Orlando and Dawn are skipping.

One hour and three thousand mosquito bites later, I'm crouched behind some elderberry bushes in back of the dock, BB gun on my lap, opera glasses hanging around my neck from a cord, waiting for the local peskies to come after the fish in the pond. I can see the fat female bass sitting on nests as the males linger a few moments in the deep before darting over, only to be chased away. Bluegill pop and smack at flies, and just as I am about to pack up and head back to the house to wait the party out, I catch sight of a fishing expedition snaking out of a stand of pines on the south side of the pond. A pair of pale, rod-toting trespassers with too tight T-shirts and Walkmans snuggled over their ears. I let them set up camp, watch them point and scheme at the breeding females sitting on nests. I think what a good thing fishing is and how I can't blame them.

But I have a job.

I figure the tall skinny one for the leader by the way he handles the fat kid. I wait for the tall one to cast before taking aim for his soft parts. The sun dips behind the trees, putting a dark spin on things. I look over my shoulder at the main house in the distance. The tiki torches are lit, music plays and I can see the tilt of headlights wandering down the drive. I wonder what sort of people come to give Warren a birthday.

I pull the trigger. The kid jumps back and drops his rod. Yelps. Fat kid quits mid-cast. I crouch. Tall and skinny fingers his belly, can't tell if the BB stuck him or stung him. He sits on the bank while I sight up the fat one. Eight pumps. Finger on trigger. Fire and he does one of those cinematic jump cuts and hits the ground squirming like a toad.

I walk around the bank toward them. My jeans pick up dew from the grass. Out in the dark of the pond bass scoot away as my shadow falls across the water. I hold the gun out in front of me, all avenging angel and shit. Skinny one sees me coming and grabs his pole.

Fat one gets brave and picks up a rock.

"You wanna rock in the head?" he sneers.

I pump the BB gun. Skinny flinches and I close in.

"This here's private property. That means no fishing," I say.

"We hear you," the skinny one says. He snaps his tackle box shut and pulls a cigarette from his shirt pocket, trying hard to be all kinds of cool.

"Fuck you," the fat one says.

I swing the gun butt at him and catch him a light one on the shoulder, just enough to let him know I mean business.

"Get out," I say.

Skinny picks himself up.

"Go on," I say, raising the gun at them again.

"Some shitty little airgun," the fat one says.

"While the getting's good," I say, with my itchy-trigger-finger look.

"And if we don't?"

I pump the gun a few times, go deadeye on the fatty until they beat a retreat through the jimson and burdock.

"We'll be back," one of them yells out of the woods.

I watch them move through the dark trees. Fireflies shoot off randomly out over the pond. I can hear the female bass slapping the water for the last of the flies. I walk back in the near-dark, gun over my shoulder, like some sort of avenging asshole.

Around midnight Mrs. Johnson buzzes me up to the house. Most of the guests are gone when I get to the backyard. Half the tiki torches have burned themselves out. Plastic cups and empty beer cans lay scattered in the grass.

"Did you get them?" she asks. She's drunk.

I nod.

"Good," she says. "Good man."

She lets slip this drunken leer that makes me quite frankly nervous in lots of ways.

“They won’t bother you no more,” I say.

She does some tawdry bullshit with her hair that starts me down some pretty dark roads.

“Well, the horse did.”

I look at her. “What horse?”

“The dead one,” she says. “Everybody smelled it.”

“I buried it,” I say.

“How deep?”

I raise my arms and jump. She shakes her head and kicks at a purple party hat.

“Not deep enough,” she says.

“I’ll move it in the morning,” I say.

“You like your job?” she says, handing me a tiki torch. All the flirt’s gone from her face. “You know where the shovels are.”

And I don’t say a word.

On my way to the shed for the shovel, she yells, “Use lime this time. It eats what’s left.”

I find the grave easy enough and there’s just enough moonlight to make the ground glow. I don’t smell a thing as I push the dirt over into a pile. When I’m a good bunch of feet down in the grave, I hear some rustling in the woods. I look up, expecting to see Mrs. Johnson or her pansy husband checking up on me. But it’s only a couple of raccoons, looking to score a little carrion. I lock eyes with the coons. They want their meat, their fair share, only there’s one problem—this salaried jackass sitting in a hole at midnight, hoping to put lime on some skin and bones.

BUFFALO

Murphy calls, says he wants to meet me down at the Chagrin River after work. "Fish and talk," he says. I can hear machines in the background, people shouting.

"When's after work?"

"I'm punching the clock now," he says. I don't hang up, because there's this pregnant silence on the other end.

"And?"

"And I have a favor to ask," he says.

I hang up, give the radio ten minutes to play something good and then leave.

On the way I buy a bottle of Dickel white label and a

sack of crushed ice, even though I'm trying to taper back a bit.

I hit the parking lot. I wait, engine on, radio off, staring at the crisp paper seal on the bottle. I can see the Chagrin snaking slow and unhurried through the gentle valley on its way to Lake Erie. The water is full of poison. Nobody eats the fish anymore, not even the homeless who camp out under the bridge in summer and fish with willow branches and shoelaces. The bums in this town wear tweed sports jackets and high-top sneakers with duct tape on them. Sometimes at night I see them walking alongside the road like deer, scrounging for returnables amid the dead dogs and trash.

I watch the cottonwood blossoms drift out into the brown river and stick in the current. Behind me under a large green-shingled pavilion city workers are installing the Frontier Days signs, pounding in log posts and tree trunks for the musket sharpshooting contest and ax throw.

Then I see Murphy's van pull in.

I wave and grab my rod out of the truck bed, reach into the cab and tuck the bottle into the bait bucket. He nods and gets out.

We walk to the river, Mayberry RFD like.

"How's the factory?" I ask.

Murphy cocks his good ear toward me—eighteen years at the same press and he's deaf in his machine-side ear. He's got gray skin, thin sand-colored hair and a bright red face that makes him look angry all the time.

"Still there," he says.

I point at the bottle. He doesn't say anything, just looks at my hands to see if they're shaking. Steady as a rock.

We go to the concrete embankment that overlooks the dam and set our gear down. I watch him rig a hook and skewer a worm. I do the same. We drop our lines into the foam, crank the drags on our reels and prop the poles against a rusty girder.

I wait ten minutes before bringing the bottle out of the bucket. I let Murphy break the seal and pour the whiskey into two coffee mugs.

I'm trying to quit, you see.

Murphy knows this, says it's a good idea, but won't tell me I shouldn't have one with him. He works—knows how it is, how a little sip or two takes the edge off, rounds off the day.

I've done the meeting thing, listened while some ex-drunk recounts his life story with a Styrofoam cup of coffee trembling in his hands. Sometimes they make me wear a name tag when I'm looking jammed up. Afterward when everybody herds together to shake hands, hug and stack foldup chairs, I just stand back against the wall until one of the old-timers shuffles over to me, slings an arm over my shoulder and asks me to join in. All the touching and good-will makes me want to jump out of my skin, especially when they tell me how I gotta fight the good fight and count the days.

I work alone and don't go out much. I fish and brood. And it's good. It's a life.

Murphy grabs his rod a minute and then sets it back down, like he just got a nibble.

"Thought I had a nibble," he says, sipping from the mug. "Thanks for coming, last minute and all."

I wave him off.

"This is good," I say.

And it is, even the river looks nice. Not like the fall coho run when the river is so full of snaggers you feel like dying. All that indelicate gear and yelling when they get a fish on, not to mention the beer cans and cigarette butts floating in the water.

I wait until Murphy looks the other way before taking the first sip.

He turns back around, eyes pinched, looking at the water. I hit him with a question, so he won't start on me about meetings and how he's happy I'm making the effort.

"How's Jeff?" I ask.

Murphy nods. It's the same nod ever since Jeff headonned a telephone pole on Lost Nation Road three years ago. He was drunk, just coming home after making last call at Delaney's Sunset Inn. There was black ice. He hit the brakes and took out some mailboxes, then the telephone pole. They pried him out of the car. The cops said he was going twenty over the limit and that he was lucky to be alive. But there was a closed head injury—one of those wait-and-see things—and he hovered in a coma for a week. When he came out of it Murphy called me from the hospital to say things were looking up and asked if I could stop by.

But Jeff wasn't right, the bleeding did a number on his brain. There were more doctors in and out of the room. One of them looked at me and said something about God rolling the dice and I wanted to punch him. Instead I got drunk and thought about going back to the hospital, waiting for the smug sonofabitch.

Jeff got fat after the accident. His hair grew back in

wild white and brown patches where they'd stitched him. Murphy had an oversized bed installed with pads in case Jeff should roll off in the middle of the night and hurt himself. During the day Jeff watched television and stared out the window as cars passed by.

"They got him on new pills. Big as my thumb," Murphy says, flipping his worm into the current, where it disappears alongside mine. "And they had a nurse come out to the house to tell me I have to put him on a better diet."

"Better diet?"

"More fiber. Less fat, all that live-to-a-hundred bullshit."

Downriver a couple of teenagers dressed in rotten sneakers and cutoffs start skipping rocks at a flock of ducks. The smell of burnt hot dogs wafts over from a noisy family picnic happening under the cottonwoods. And it's a family photo: Dad doing battle with the yellow jackets, while Mom watches her three children run along the tops of the picnic tables throwing water at each other from red plastic cups.

"What's the favor?" I ask, steadying my hands against the concrete. For a minute the sound of the river breaking over the dam fills my head. He clears his throat and fiddles with the drag setting on his reel.

"Well, Jeff saw one of them stupid ads on the television for Frontier Days. They got these spots with a bunch of guys running around the woods in buckskin pants and long rifles."

I look at him, shrug my shoulders.

"They're on during the Tribe games. In between innings—you've seen them."

"I guess I haven't," I say.

"Well, Jeff likes them," he says. "Keeps telling me how he wants to go, wants to see the ax toss and buffalo stampede."

"I thought the mayor nixed the buffalo this year."

"I don't think so," he says. "Anyway. I've got to work this Saturday."

Just then one of the kids from the picnic table approaches the embankment and tosses a hot dog into the water. The hot dog eddies in the current before sinking and leaving an oily trail of mustard floating on the water. The father murmurs an apology and Murphy waves him off.

"Can't you call in sick?" I ask.

Murphy shakes his head and checks his line to find that most of his worm has been nibbled off.

"We're short as it is. Betty Brownlow quit and got married. Can't get the God squadders to work the weekends and foreman Frank's pissing and moaning about meeting some deadline. Hell, I promised them."

"So you need me . . ." I start.

"I wouldn't ever ask, but I tried Mrs. Evers already."

My hands tremble as I watch Murphy bait his hook again.

"I'll have to put off a little job I got going," I lie. Murphy licks his lips and runs his fingers through his thinning hair. "I know it's a lot to ask, but he's seen the goddamn commercials on the television and I can't get him to stop talking about it. He's got it in his head to see a live buffalo. It would mean a lot to him."

"No problem," I say. "Does he remember me?"

"Sure he does," Murphy says excitedly. "Just don't touch him, remember that."

"You sure about this?"

"You'd be doing me one big favor," he says.

I don't say a word. The river hisses and snakes around logs and rocks, kids scream in the distance and after a few minutes it's just us fishing again and everything is normal. Then the sun starts to go down and I can feel the damp air dropping off the hills. I don't dare have another drink in front of Murphy, so I fill up his mug, screw the cap back on the bottle and tuck it into the bucket where I can't see it.

"You can pick him up in the morning," Murphy says.

"No problem," I say. I pull my line against the current and then let it drift.

When Saturday rolls around I haven't had a drop in three days. My face feels like it wants to peel off. My hands hurt. I pull on my clothes and stir together some breakfast. Murphy calls me from the plant. I can hear the presses in the background. He has to shout. Says he wants to remind me that Jeff knows I'm coming and that it was all he could talk about last night. He tries to thank me again and I tell him to forget it, that it'll be fun and everything will be okay. A promise is a promise and all that.

The last time I went to Frontier Days was with this woman named Marie who got drunk on peach schnapps and threw up on the Roto-Twirl. I was out of work then and crazy from sitting around on my hands, waiting for the phone to ring. I never saw her again. Then I got work and was too busy to even think about her, just the money fluttering in from the jobs and the promise of a drink after the tools were put away. I had life in a box. There was no future, just each day, one at a time. I started kicking things around, looking at my options, like some sort of high noon of the soul. Only it happened every day and I was the hero for slogging it out, never getting wiser like the Christians and smart fuckers in their BMWs with their blonde arm-candy wives and squirmy children. Instead of charting a course I spent a lot of time deciding what I didn't want to be, drinking toasts to this and that, getting by. But then nothing happened. I am still a carpenter.

At the meetings there's this old huggy bastard named Baron who helped build city hall back when they did all the figuring in their heads. Baron says he used to drink two bottles of beer after work. He felt good about where his life was going. Then it was six and from there it was a hop, skip and a jump to twelve and the bottle. When he asks me if I keep count I pretend not to hear, because he's old and full of that clean and sober energy.

I drive over to Murphy's house, a small two-bedroom bungalow with a nice dogwood tree in the front yard. There are still some flowers left over from Murphy's ex-wife, Katrina, who went on sudden gardening binges the year before she left him, planting bulbs all over the place, mulching everything, even the light post.

But since her departure Murphy has managed to neglect or mow over most of the once burgeoning flower beds, leaving only a few yellow daylilies and some anemic-looking gladiolus.

I ring the bell and wait until the door swings open. Jeff stands behind the glass storm door, staring at me blankly for a minute like a bank teller. He's taller than me, pear-shaped. His hair looks as if somebody else has combed it. I wave and he smiles before opening the door. I forget and extend a hand for him to shake. He looks at me and puts his hand behind his back.

"Can I go now?" he asks. He shuffles closer. "Dad says I go see buffalo right now."

"Sure," I say.

"Right now."

His brown eyes, still crusted with sleep, stare at my mouth and then at my hands. Not so steady with those three days. I get nervous and clap a few times and tell him to saddle up. He jumps up and down, patting his hair and shifting his weight from side to side.

He settles and then goes to the door, opens it carefully and peers outside, like there are snipers waiting for him.

I point at the truck.

"You still want to go?" I ask, hoping he'll shake his head no and that will be it. Favor extended. Favor refused. But I've already sunk three days into this for Murphy, so I point at the truck again.

"Sure, yeah," he slurs. "Very cool, very cool—I go."

I step out into the sunlight and head toward the truck. He follows.

I buckle his seat belt for him. He stiffens when I touch him and sits there staring out through the windshield like he's remembering his accident all over again. Then I show him how the radio works. He punches the buttons from station to station. "I like them all now," he says, his voice flat and spooky. I try to remember what he was like before the accident. He was just another young thug, learning to drink and lie, generally up to no good with no strong feeling either way on criminal behavior. And now he's got nurses coming over, feeding him pills, talking about his diet. You tell me what's the better shake—what would have happened or what did happen?

I let him roll down the window and stick his head out like a dog. The wind whips his face into a smile and for a moment he's pure joy. Suddenly he pulls his head in like somebody turned off the wind. There is a wasp stuck in his hair. It flexes its wing a moment before shooting out the window to freedom.

"We're going to Frontier Days," I say, trying to put some party in the line.

"Dad told me. Buffalo, they going to shoot the buffalo and I'm gonna watch."

"They won't shoot the buffalo," I say. "They're for people to look at."

My hands are shaking again and I'm talking too loud.

"You say, whatever," he says as we dip into the river valley and turn off at the Daniel's Park sign. A huge banner that reads FRONTIER DAYS has been strung across two elm trees. Jeff stops punching the radio button and stares out the window at the banner as a policeman in an orange vest points his flashlight to direct us down a dirt path behind some other cars. Several families waddle by armed with foldup lawn chairs and coolers. The kids carry unlit sparklers and miniature American flags in tight pink fists. Jeff stays quiet, watches the people stream by as I look for something to come across his face, anything, a smile or frown. But there is nothing.

We park and pile out. Jeff stretches and stares at the noon time sun. Off in the distance I can hear the echo of gunshots and cheers. A fat man in a buckskin jacket crashes out of a blue Porta-John, buckling his pants. Jeff stops stretching and stares.

"Davy fucking Crockett," he says, pointing.

The man glares at us, his eyes full of beer and maybe too many hours of work. He's got hands like a welder and one of those I-ride-a-Harley beards.

"Problem?" he says to Jeff.

Jeff freezes, crazy smile plastered across his face, drool coming in buckets.

"He's . . ." I start, but the man nods.

"I understand," he says, walking away. Jeff makes a gun with his fingers and shoots the man in the back, laughs and then falls silent again. He wanders over to the river and stands there on the muddy bank, head bowed.

That's when I start looking for the beer garden tent.

"We can come back and look at the water later," I say, hoping he doesn't jump in after something and drown.

He turns, stares at me and for a moment I realize he has no clue who I am—just this guy hustling him away from the river to get to some beer.

I walk back up through the crowd and he follows until we are under the bright yellow-and-white canvas of the beer tent. I buy a string of tickets and order a beer, sip off the warm foam and give Jeff two tickets. He carefully takes the tickets without touching my hand and orders a Coke. He gulps it down and burps loudly. The counter girl looks at me and smiles. There are hickeys on her neck and plenty of split ends framing her pale face.

"More," Jeff says. She pours him another, less ice this time. He drinks it down and leaves.

We move through the crowd. Nobody steps in front of Jeff. One look at his checked-out expression and people move the other way and whisper.

Jeff follows the gunshots and comes to a small field lined with brown snow fence. Families sit on wool blankets and lawn chairs. The children watch as men and women dressed like pathfinders load muskets on rickety plywood tables. The air is thick with black powder and wet grass. A chubby woman in an old-fashioned lace dress stands on a riser, waving her handkerchief at the shooters.

"Gentlemen," she says. "Load your weapons."

Two old-timers dressed in pin-striped shirts and derby hats stand near the targets ready to tally scores on a marker board. Jeff stares at the guns a minute before making his way to the front of the crowd yelling "excuse me" in people's ears. I follow him, apologizing in his wake, knowing there's not enough beer in the world to make this any easier.

Somebody whoops and throws an empty beer cup onto the field as the rifles fire and gray-blue smoke drifts out over the crowd. The old-timers go to the targets and dig around with pencils and yell out who hit what.

When I catch up to Jeff he is pressed up against the yellow divider rope and snow fence watching the men in buckskin slip ramrods down into their rifles. A woman dressed in a coonskin cap and shooting gloves with long ribbons of brown fringe looks at us and says, "Howdy."

Jeff says howdy back, just long and flat enough for her to suspect that something's wrong. She looks at me like I'm his father and smiles politely before loading her gun.

"Shoot," Jeff yells. He laughs and pats his hair.

A little girl dressed in a Mickey Mouse T-shirt and yellow shorts points at Jeff, shaking a piece of watermelon at him. Her mother leans over and tells her to eat the melon and not to play with it. The girl stomps her feet and throws the wedge of melon on the ground. Jeff stares at the melon in the dirt until the crack of rifles breaks his attention.

We watch the contest. Lady Buckskin hits a bull's-eye and bows to the crowd, blowing kisses. Two other men take aim with mirrors over their shoulders and fire. Afterward, they hold the mirrors up to the crowd. Jeff cranes his neck to see himself in the mirror, pushing his belly tight against the rope as I drain the rest of my beer, not quite sure what to do or say.

This is easy, I tell myself.

Just as I start thinking about another beer the little girl in the Mickey Mouse T-shirt approaches Jeff again and taps him on the knee. He freezes and starts yelling, "Hot, hot, hot, hot!" His arms shoot down to his sides and the girl runs away crying.

"Sorry," I say to the girl's mother. I give her some parental shorthand that tells her Jeff is not right.

Jeff stops screaming when the lady in the dress calls out for the shooters to shoot and the loaders to load. I think about Murphy punching the button on his press, worrying about Jeff and sweating the time clock.

"Want another Coke?" I ask him. He nods and begins walking toward the beer tent, yelling "excuse me" loud enough to shake up this old couple having a go at some cotton candy.

We make the beer tent and stand in line. Jeff rocks back and forth, one foot then the other, humming the theme to *Sesame Street.*

A woman bumps into me from behind. I turn around and look into eyes so brown my heart stops beating for a minute and my throat goes dry. Her hair is long, the color of fresh asphalt. She has on loose khaki shorts and a white muscle T-shirt.

"Sorry," she says, placing a hand on my shoulder. I can smell the beer on her breath. There's nobody with her and I start thinking about getting lucky when Jeff turns around and burps at us.

She laughs.

"Yours?" she asks, tapping an empty beer cup against her hips.

"Sort of and not really," I tell her.

She bites her lower lip and laughs again. "Which is it?"

"I'm doing a favor for my buddy," I tell her. Then I lean into her so Jeff can't hear. "He was in an accident. Scrambled him some."

She nods and looks at me over her empty beer glass.

"You want another one?" I ask.

"If you're buying," she says.

"All day," I say, showing her my string of tickets.

"You bet," she says.

Jeff sees the tickets. "Ooh," he says, rubbing his stomach. I hand him a few.

"You look familiar. You ever go to meetings?"

"Depends what kind," I say. "And who's asking."

"Wanda," she says. "And you know what I'm talking about."

I nod. "I go sometimes."

"I thought I recognized you," Wanda says.

"My name's Dan." I extend a hand for her to shake.

"We're not supposed to be doing this," she says, pointing at the beer glasses. "But my divorce papers just came through and I live just up the street and you know what?"

"What?"

"I got tired of hearing the people having fun. And what the hell—how many times you get divorced?"

"Not many, I hope."

We watch Jeff order another Coke. He places two tickets on the counter carefully and then jerks his hand back before pointing at the soda machine.

"How come you never talk at the meetings?" she asks. "Me, I just let it all out and I don't give a damn what any of them thinks."

"I don't really have a problem," I say.

"Sure," she says. "Neither do I."

"It's not like that."

"Don't worry, I won't tell. Me—I'm kissing three months good-bye and I've never felt better. What's the longest for you?"

"I told you," I say. "It's not like that."

"Okay," she says. "We can play that game."

"Deal," I say.

She pauses, rolls her eyes. I can see she's had too many.

"You ought to talk more at the meetings," she says. "People are beginning to wonder about you."

"That's okay with me."

"The mystery man," she says, shaking that brown hair.

I buy her another beer and when I turn around to hand it to her she says, "Your friend—he just walked off."

I search the crowd looking for his slump shoulders and crazy hair and it's as if he's vanished.

"Did you see where he went?" I ask, trying not to panic.

"He took off that way when you weren't looking. C'mon, we'll find him," she says, taking my hand and leading me through the crowd.

We check the ax and hatchet throw, the midway. No Jeff. I start thinking about Murphy and begin jogging. Wanda follows, apologizing as I race over to the corn-roasting pit. By the time we hit the midway again I am running. I hear voices bark out names of games, Three Darts, Three Balloons—One Buck, Dunk the Clown.

We walk back to the river and still no Jeff. Wanda takes a look at me and I can see the fear registering in her eyes, making her sober.

"This wasn't supposed to happen. I'm responsible for him. I promised his father."

"Maybe he went back to the car?"

"Where are the buffalo?" I ask her.

"Over there," she says, lifting a few damp strands of hair from her neck.

I take her hand and lead her through the crowd.

The buffalo pen is past the Tilt-A-Whirl under a patch

of scraggly-looking poplars. We smell them first—a sun-baked stew of wet carpet, dead dog and buffalo shit.

"There's a man out there with the buffalo," I hear somebody say. My tongue drops back into my lungs.

Wanda sees him first and gasps. Several rent-a-cops and a police officer are circling a small herd of dusty-looking buffalo. The officer has his revolver drawn while the rent-a-cops brandish flashlights.

Then I see Jeff. He is standing inside the pen surrounded by the animals, his red Cleveland Indians T-shirt visible against the dirty brown fur. A man dressed in buckskins is talking through a bullhorn at him, his words breaking in choppy amplified waves I can't make out.

I push my way to the front of the crowd and see Jeff waving his arms, as if he is orchestrating some private dance with the buffalo as they mill around him. I hop the fence and pull Wanda over. Her shorts catch on a stave iron and tear.

"Shit," she says, dark, sweaty hair cascading around her face as she steadies herself against me. "Just my luck."

"He's going to get killed," I say.

"Please remain behind the fence," a rent-a-cop says as he intercepts us, pointing a heavy steel flashlight at my chest like a gun.

"His name's Jeff," I tell him.

Wanda nods and grabs my hand, laces her fingers through mine and squeezes. The rent-a-cop lowers the flashlight, his hands shaking slightly.

"Are you with him?" the rent-a-cop asks, pointing to the animals.

"He's not right," I say.

"What was your first clue?" he says. His face starts turning red at the edges. Sweat boils out of his pores, runs down his neck soaking his tight collar.

I glare at him and clench my jaw.

"I'm sorry," he stammers, tossing his hands into the air. "It's just we've got a real situation here."

One of the police officers steps away from the ring of onlookers and approaches us. "You know that man?" the officer asks, pointing at Jeff. His face is webbed with broken vessels and his nose looks as if it has been broken more than a few times.

I nod. "His name's Jeff and he doesn't really know what he's doing."

Wanda squeezes my hand.

"Can you get him to come out of there?" he asks. "That's all I need to know."

"I can try."

"We've got somebody looking for the farmer who brought the animals, see if maybe he's got any ideas," he says.

"Can't you walk in and get him?" I ask.

"We tried that. He started yelling, said he was going to shoot or something. We think maybe he's got a gun."

"He don't have a gun," I say tightly.

"I don't want to be the one to find out," the officer says. "And I don't want to get stampeded or anyone else for that matter."

"He just wants to see the animals."

"Yeah, but that don't fix our problem, now does it? He

gets himself hurt, the city's liable. Are you gonna take responsibility for that?"

"I'll get him," I say.

"As long as nobody gets hurt," he says. "I don't want to have to start shooting buffalo and upset the kids."

I walk out to where the buffalo are pinched into a tight herd. All the grass has been worn away from their hooves. The noise of the crowd drops away like I'm in some sort of box. Jeff sees me coming and starts waving.

When I'm near the outside edge of the herd I put my hands out in front of me and close my eyes. I wait until the ground stops shaking before opening my eyes. Three feet in front of me stands one of the larger buffalo. It shakes its mane at me and stomps, causing the whole herd to shift about nervously. I take a few more steps, figuring there are only two ways to come out of this mess: dead or injured.

I move slowly, touching the animals on the sides, guiding them away from me until one of them leans its rump into me and I can feel every muscle in its body quiver.

Jeff wades further into the brown mass, daring me to follow him through the animals, who look at me with these round unblinking eyes. Several of them lower their horns as I pass by, touching their dirty flanks. I glance over my shoulder to find Wanda but she's lost in the crowd pressed against the fence.

When I get within ten feet of Jeff a pair of buffalo step in front of me, their heads lowered as if at a moment's notice they are ready to stomp me to death.

"Go now," Jeff says, patting an animal on the back as it leans into him. I edge around to the other side and again the animals react and block my path as if they're guarding him.

"Don't shoot them," Jeff says.

"It's Dan," I say. "Nobody's going to shoot anything."

He shakes his head. One of the animals starts licking his leg, it's long rough tongue rasping against his Levi's. Jeff's face lights into a grin. I see how delicate the whole thing is, how maybe he moves too fast or hits one of them and the whole herd charges the fences, trampling trash barrels, scattering pylons and crushing children.

But he doesn't.

He lets the animal keep licking and I work my way through the last wall of animals until I am standing beside him.

"Steady," I say. Jeff looks at me and shakes his head. I can hear the crowd now. Little children screaming and pointing; drunks yelling out advice. I shut my ears and put out a hand for him. The buffalo at his side stops licking and looks at me. Jeff stares at my hand. I hold my breath and inch toward him like I'm going after somebody stuck in the ice. The breeze picks up and lifts the stink of animals away for a moment, allowing the scent of warm summer river water and cotton candy to drift across us. The animals shift nervously, and before I know it, I am surrounded by them, my chest filled with the sound of their hooves pounding the ground.

I move closer to Jeff and just when I can almost touch him he wraps his arms around one of the buffalo. For a minute I expect the whole herd to move in one merciless brown swarm, tramping me like grass. But they don't.

The animal just stands there as Jeff presses his face into

its neck and smells. I touch his back. He ignores me and keeps on hugging. The animal's eye rolls in my direction and for a moment I don't know what to do. I take my hand off Jeff and just watch them for a minute. The bullhorn cackles more words I can't understand. Muskets crack and split the air in the distance. Jeff looks at me, his face covered with fur and dirt, and for the first time today I recognize someone in his eyes, like maybe he remembers he was getting old once, waiting to fall in love, planning the rest of his life. I watch him squeeze harder and harder, his face buried against the animal, like this is what he needs, what he came for and he doesn't care about what happens after, because it's too important for that.

All around me the animals begin nudging and pushing me out of the circle, closing ranks. I start thinking of Murphy then and what I'm going to tell him. I look at Jeff in the sea of brown, hugging tighter and tighter, holding as if his whole life has been smashed down to this bright diamond of a moment and he doesn't care if it blows up or twitches to bad, because he's got his arms wrapped around three thousand pounds of life and death.

HAPPY JACK

Three nights a week I teach a women's self-defense course at the YWCA. My students are mostly middle-aged women, ten to fifteen pounds overweight—normal everyday women with varicose veins, sagging breasts and dimpled thighs. They are tired and want something more from their lives besides cooking chili mac and looking after screaming children.

My class is not that something.

So what if I am no more qualified than the next guy to teach self-defense to a bunch of scared and lonely housewives? I lied and got the job and there are moments, when I am looking out over my class as they struggle with leg raises, thigh muscles jiggling with pain, waiting for me to give them the ten count, that this deep sense of happiness comes over me and I think to myself that I am blessed among men.

I don't believe in all that karate and kung-fu bullshit. What I give my students is good old commonsense advice. I tell them to avoid dark parking lots and being alone. And they want to hear this. Because nobody wants to be alone, especially women. Because to be alone is to be afraid and to be afraid is a terrible thing—something we must defend ourselves against.

I have them do jumping jacks and push-ups from their knees as I walk around the gym's wooden floor, counting out the reps, listening to them grunt and sweat. After warm-up I go into the equipment closet and pull on my attack suit, a heavy canvas thing with padding everywhere, sweat stains in the armpits and a bell-shaped helmet with reflectors over the eyeholes. The real gem of the suit is this small battery-operated reflector unit in the crotch that the previous instructor installed shortly before his departure. The unit is rigged so that any direct hit causes it to light up and flash like a fire engine.

In the cramped men's locker room there are several framed photographs of my predecessor, Gordon, standing in front of graduating classes of women. He is an avuncular-looking man with chest hair popping out of the collar of his shirt and leathery skin that reminds me of why too much sun is a bad thing. Two months ago when I applied for the job, I was told that he'd quit to join the Scientologists and later moved to Utah with his third wife, a former student. It was the former student part that got him trouble.

I met Mary Renfrew, the Y's director of activities, on my second interview. Mary is a burly woman on the downside of forty and has one of those broad, unhappy faces that seem to always be wincing or squinting at something in the distance—the sort of woman that if you passed her on the street you wouldn't think twice about.

I followed her into her office. My hands were sweating and I was having a hard time breathing. I needed the job.

"Sit down," she said, pointing at a rickety maple chair that sat just beneath a tattered poster of Billie Jean King frozen midstroke, her jaw set firmly, forearms rippling with effort. "I'm looking for a people person," she said. "Somebody who shares the Y's vision. Not one of these Johnny-come-latelies."

I shifted uncomfortably in my chair and watched as she tugged her striped tube socks up around her flabby knees.

"You mean?"

"I mean situations may arise," she said. "This is, after all, a coed facility, not like the YMCA across town, but we do have our share of men."

"I have a girlfriend," I lied. She stared at me, fingering the worn brass whistle that hung around her neck. I felt Billie Jean's disapproving gaze and I knew that Mary was most probably a lesbian and that she too was surrounded by temptation.

"Do we understand each other, Mr. Lamarr?" she asked.

"Do I have the job?" I said.

She twisted her face at me until it resembled something close to a smile.

"Welcome aboard," she said. Then the smile dropped from her face as quickly as it had appeared. She reached into a drawer in her desk and handed me a thin blue booklet.

"Look this over," she said.

I asked her what it was.

"Rules and regulations. There aren't many male instructors here," she said. "Besides, I don't want another Gordon on my hands. That little incident caused quite a stir with the board of directors."

"You can trust me," I said.

She laughed and showed me to the door. "I don't trust anybody," she said. "Least as far as I can throw them. That's why we have rules and regulations."

I thanked her and wandered out through the chlorine-scented halls into the daylight, happy to have a job, when I was sure she'd gone back into her office I dropped the rule book into a garbage can overflowing with candy wrappers and smashed wax cups.

Now, whenever I see a woman slapping barefoot down the hall, Speedo riding high on her hips and broad midwestern smile plastered across her face, I think of Mary Renfrew's flabby knees and of Gordon in Utah with his third wife and I look away. But I am not always so good and pure and sometimes I linger around the pool area, admiring the self-conscious swell of a mother's shoulders as she lifts herself out of the deep end and looks around before pulling her suit down over her hips or tucking in a stray breast. I finger my plastic name plate that announces me as an official instructor and pretend to look at the trophy case. But there are women everywhere. The neatly tiled hallways are full of their smells: talcum powder, hand lotion and sweat. And I know that I will somehow manage to screw this job up.

I begin the course by telling my students that the most effective way to stop a would-be attacker, when all else has failed, is to aim for the groin. They titter and laugh into their hands and talk among themselves. I feel awkward and out of place standing before them, because what I really want for them is to never have to be in a position to defend themselves. But the newspapers are full of reports of attacks, rapes and abusive husbands and they've paid their membership dues and registration fee for the class. So I teach them the proper way to punch and kick, show them how to exhale and scream when they strike. I raise my arms menacingly and let them kick me with everything that is not quite right in their lives—the dirty diapers, half-full beer cans left to ring end tables, expired coupons, stretch marks, phone solicitors, husbands who sit on La-Z-Boys watching football and that little paunch that happens after the second child that won't go away no matter how many sit-ups they do. They kick and hurt me and I understand because it is my job.

On Monday I pretend to be a would-be rapist. I stand a couple of mats up like walls and creep around the corner in my suit, making Darth Vader sounds through the face mask. A few of the volleyballers on the other side of the gym laugh and make jokes as Fran Darden sends me to the floor with a heavy kick and a few punches just like I have taught her. I congratulate her on her form and she lights up, sashaying to the back of the line, her broad hips and chubby arms shaking with excitement as the rest of the girls high-five her. Jill Olsten is next and she forgets to finish me off with a claw to my eye reflectors.

"Jill," I say, pointing to my head.

"Ohh," she says, biting her lower lip. "I forgot."

I line her up again and come around the corner, arms raised, breathing heavy like some desperate lust mad assailant.

"Get the bastard!" Fran says from the back of the line. Several others hoot and cheer. This time Jill kicks me in the crotch twice with her heel. The reflector unit goes haywire and she stands over me, her jaw clenched tightly, fists pumping the air, as I roll to my feet for the next one.

On Wednesday we watch a video on parking lot safety. Most of it's crap—terrible production values, illegible titles, to say nothing of the actors who look like out-of-work porn stars. But Mary has ordered the videos special for the class, so I show them. This one is particularly bad. The actor playing the attacker is a hard-won fifty and potbellied. He looks like Captain Kangaroo after a bender, as he bumbles around several parked cars, hairpiece shifting in the wind. Sharon Oates, a skinny, shy woman with hair the color of carrots, says the man reminds her of her ex-husband. Fran, the self-appointed mother of the group, puts an arm around her shoulder and coos, "Poor baby."

Sharon watches and sighs as the man throws his flabby arms out, lunging like a professional wrestler at this pale actress in a wrinkled business suit. The woman ducks and the man misses, bouncing off her Eldorado just in time to catch a high heel to his upper thigh.

After the video, I feign a car assault on Diane Dross. She rakes my face mask with a fistful of keys and follows up with a series of kicks and knee thrusts which catch me in the spleen and send me flopping to the mat.

On my list of women whom I'd most like to see naked, Diane is number one. She speaks four languages and has three children, named Tommy, Joe and Belinda. She has thick maple-colored hair and long red nails, one of which has a real diamond stuck through a hole in it. She is the kind of woman men are both afraid of and crazy for. And I am no exception.

Whenever she talks to me she touches my arm and I feel good all over, like I'm underwater and there is blue sky above me. But there is the job and my promise to Mary Renfrew, not to mention Gordon somewhere in Utah.

To make matters worse, Diane is happily married. Her husband, Charlie, forecloses on loans 9:00 to 4:30 five days a week at Great Lakes Bank. I hate him even though I have never met him.

Sometimes Diane stays behind and we talk, long after the rest of the class has hit the showers. I tell her about my life before this. How I had a little place in the Florida Keys, taught scuba diving and loved a woman named Tina. Things looked sunny and bright. But then two students croaked and I had to leave.

Diane listens and in a perfect world she would be mine,

but in this world I settle for the two of us talking in an empty gym and her touching my arm.

Two weeks ago she told me about this man who had his house taken away from him by her husband. I was out of my suit, and Diane was practicing her elbow thrust, which required me to bear hug her. She said that the man would call their house late at night and say bad things to her. "And that's why you're taking this course?" I asked.

"Maybe," she said, pressing her teeth against her bottom lip as she followed up the elbow with a near-perfect knee thrust to my chest.

"You can't hurt me," I said, rolling up from the mat.

"Don't be so sure, Mr. Happy Jack. There are more than a few ways to hurt a man."

I smiled and positioned myself behind her, wrapped my arms around her. It was all so easy. I was her teacher. The gym was empty and I could smell her hair and feel the slick of sweat on her shoulders. Then I heard the clomp of Mary coming around the corner, bouncing a red, white and blue basketball. The dribbling stopped, and for a moment we locked eyes—she squinting, me not there at all. Then Diane struck, screaming as she rammed her elbow into my sternum. I went down holding my stomach and Mary started dribbling again, happy to see me in pain and not in a social way with one of my students.

"You owe me," Diane said as she helped me to my feet. "I just saved your job."

I nodded and watched her walk off to the showers. Already I could feel a bruise forming under my rib cage where she'd hit me. One of the janitors came in and began clicking off the lights. I sat there for a long time in the darkness, thinking about how Diane and her go-getter husband, Charlie, and had a corner on the happiness market. I wanted Diane to come back and let me hold her—no punching or kicking this time. Only there are rules, and I am her instructor—a people person and I am thirty-five years old, never married and living here in the Midwest. I have a student who calls me Happy Jack and touches my arm.

On Friday when I walk into the gym, the class is already assembled on the far side, and for once there are no volleyball players.

"Hello, class," I say.

"Hey, Jack," they say.

I look at Diane and she winks at me. I smile and retrieve the body armor from the equipment closet and drag it out onto the mats as if it were a dead person. I get the class started on jumping jacks and then some kicks. Diane is in her skimpy cotton number and I can see her belly button when she stretches. I remind myself that I must show her no more attention than the next woman. So I walk over and stare at Mrs. Tuchovny's spastic kicks until the sight of Diane's belly button fades.

After they're warmed up I say, "Today we're going to work on personal space."

"How personal?" Diane taunts. Everybody laughs.

"You made him blush," Fran Darden says. "Isn't that cute?"

I wait for them to quiet down before summoning Selma Schwartz from the front row and telling her to stand next to me. Selma is a large nervous woman who moves as if she is in constant danger of breaking something.

"Like this?" she asks. I nod approvingly and ask the class what they would do if a stranger suddenly tried to grab them. Then I demonstrate on Selma, raising my arms in front of me like Boris Karloff as Frankenstein chasing down the girl with the flowers. I want to scare her, let her know how real this could be and that she shouldn't roll over and be the perfect victim, that I have taught her to save herself or go down fighting. Instead Selma panics and nearly falls.

"Run," someone says. But Selma is still trying to regain her balance.

"Okay," I say, motioning Selma back into position. "What if you can't run?"

"You smash him," Mrs. Tuchovny says.

"Smash where?" I ask.

The class is silent for a minute until Diane steps up to the front and places her palm on my throat.

"Here," she says.

Her hand is smooth and warm and I start sweating. "Good," I say. "Selma?"

Selma looks at me and nods.

"How would you do it?" I ask.

Diane pulls her hand away. "Like this," she says, swinging the heel of her palm toward my face. I flinch and Diane giggles and goes back to her place in line, leaving me all alone with Selma in front of the class.

"Okay, Selma," I say, slightly rattled by Diane's touch. "You can get back in line."

Selma lets out a long sigh and waddles back to her place in line, happy to be out of the spotlight.

Then I put on the suit and tell them to practice their kicks. They take aim and for five minutes I am kicked, scratched, batted and pawed. Shirley Thanos goes eight-for-eight on my crotch, red lights every time. And after a while the desire is beaten out of me. I am the man in the mask—whatever bad thing they want me to be.

I end class with another video, and nobody says much of anything. Diane doesn't hang around after; instead she darts off to the locker room with the rest of the women. I wait for her to return and when she doesn't I put the television and video player away, stack the mats in the corner and go out to the parking lot without showering. I put the key in the ignition and watch as women go to their minivans, clicking keyless-entry devices, shifting duffel bags over tired shoulders.

I wait until Diane comes out, her hair streaming behind her like a wet cape, long red nails catching the streetlamp glare. She climbs into her Lexus without looking around her—something I've warned the whole class never to do—and roars off.

And I follow. It is that easy. I just slip into traffic behind her. She drives down a series of side streets, the houses getting larger as the address numbers descend. I open the window and the moist, heavy air reminds me of Diane's hand on my throat.

Finally she slows the Lexus and makes a right-hand turn into a drive that leads to a dark three-story house. Small lights line the drive like a runway. The yard looks black and full of trees. I drive around the corner and park next to a small playground circled by Cyclone fencing. A dog barks somewhere as I walk slowly toward Diane's house, palms sweating.

I walk straight down her driveway and head for a large oak tree that looms over the house, splashing it with an even darker shade of night. There are windows everywhere. Abandoned bicycles and plastic buckets dot the yard. I close my eyes, and when I open them I am staring into a room illuminated by a narrow strip of light coming from somewhere out in the hallway. The room is bare, save for a plant stand with a sick-looking fern perched atop it and a carved armchair in the opposite corner. I move around to the back of the house, shoes picking up dew from the grass. I come to a bathroom. Everything is white, even the bath mat. There are towels hanging from white porcelain hooks on the back of the door, toothbrushes under the mirror, pill bottles and a hairbrush with long hairs twilled through its teeth—Diane's hairs, I think. Or perhaps her daughter's. I put my hand to the glass and let out a breath as a shadow darkens the hallway and then passes. I can hear people inside, but I can't see them. I keep moving and come to a set of double glass doors that open onto a wooden deck. Leaning against the deck, I can see into the kitchen. It is also empty. Then I see my distorted reflection in the glass.

I wait. It's as if Diane and her happy family have retreated to some heart of the house that I will never be able to see into. After a minute I sneak around to the other side. There are no trees, only a few shrubs, but I find the family room. The television is on, the couch empty; a puzzle lies scattered across the thick Oriental rug, a suit jacket slung over the back of a chair. I press my forehead against the window, and that's when I see her come padding into the room. It is Diane's daughter, and she is in her Snoopy pajamas, ratty-looking teddy bear tucked under her arm. She looks just like her mother, only softer and the sight of her frail body overlapped with my ghostlike reflection in the glass makes me realize, a moment too late, what I have done. Just when I am about to turn and go she sees me.

I watch it all in the reflection—the little girl and me, the strange man, with my desire—hoping to see what?

For a minute neither of us moves. Then the teddy bear hits the floor. Her mouth opens. "No," I say. "No, please." I hold up a finger, but it's too late, and I feel the scream before I hear it. I stumble backward, tripping on a rhododendron bush, landing face-first in the bark mulch, before regaining my feet and scrambling down the driveway.

I run past mazelike hedges and fake split-rail fences until I am lost. There are no couples out for nightly walks or people with dogs on leashes. Just empty streets and well-lighted houses.

Finally I spot a car and run after it, hoping to get directions, the little girl's scream still ringing in my ear. The car slows for a moment and I can see the driver checking the rearview mirror before speeding off. I walk and walk and nothing looks familiar. Then I hear the purr of an engine in the distance. I follow the engine sound around a corner to see a large white truck with two yellow tanks mounted to its back idling in front of a two story colonial. Bright orange caution signs hang from a series of shiny rods just above the bumper. An even larger sign on the side reads:

DANGER MOSQUITO CONTROL SPRAY—KEEP SAFE DISTANCE AND AVOID FUMES.

The truck pulls away from the curb and begins making its way down the street slowly. The pipes and rods come to life, blanketing the pavement behind it with this beautiful white cloud. I keep running anyway, thinking if I can only ask directions I'll be okay—that I will stop following students home and looking in their windows because of the way they touch my arm or the color of their hair or because I want to and I am lonely.

But the poison seems to crawl out of the hedges and grass, enveloping me in its wake until my eyes begin to water and my nose burns. The truck pulls farther away and I stop running. A steady rain of dead bugs falls out of the sky like ash. This is the consequence of desire, I think, to be lost, lonely and poisoned. The truck disappears around the corner and I start walking until the moon slips behind a cloud, and just when my lungs begin to clear and the sour taste leaves my mouth, my car suddenly appears in the distance.

When I get back to my room I sleep and watch television for two days. I think of Diane and see her daughter screaming at me, a stranger in the window—the teddy bear crashing to the floor—and I know I've done damage to their happy home and that I will have to face her in class and she won't know—can't know—that it was me.

On the night of my class, I take a long shower, shave and go to Denny's and eat a Grand Slam Special before heading down to the Y. I tell myself that I must go on as if nothing has happened. I am the instructor. I will be in front of the class and Diane will be there and it will be okay until I have to touch her.

On my way to the locker room, Mary steps out of her office and invites me in. She smiles as I take a seat under the watchful gaze of the Billie Jean King poster. She's in a chatty mood and asks me how I'm getting along.

"Fine," I say.

"One of your students," she says, pausing to look about the room.

I cringe, half expecting her to chew me out or fire me.

"Yes," I say.

"One of your students came up to me the other day and wanted to say what a great job you were doing, that you took them seriously."

"Really?"

"That's all," she says. Her face scrunches back up. "I just thought you would appreciate the feedback. It's always nice to know when you're doing a good job."

"Don't believe a word of it," I say. She laughs and that's how I leave her, thinking what a great funny guy I am.

In the locker room, I get dressed and then go out to the gym. My class is waiting and there are volleyball players on the other side of the gym. When one of their balls rolls in front of me, I kick it.

Diane is in the front row and she looks tired and I know that is because of me and what her daughter saw.

"Okay, class," I say. "Let's warm up."

We do exercises and after ten minutes it's like it's always been, except that I can't stop looking at Diane, wondering if she's the one who put in a good word for me or if she knows I was outside her house.

I pull on the suit.

"Okay," I say. "I'm in your home and I've just surprised you coming in from the den. There is a brief struggle, ending with me holding you from behind."

"Ooh, Jack, you're scaring us," Fran Darden says.

I ignore her and continue. "I'm in your house. I've got you from behind."

The class goes quiet a moment and I do not look at Diane.

Finally Jill Olsten raises her hand. "Do we elbow or kick first?" she asks.

"First you drop your center of gravity," I say as I prepare to wrap my arms around a quivering Selma.

"Center of gravity?" Mrs. Tuchovny says.

"He means your hips, honey," Diane says.

Mrs. Tuchovny makes a fist and shakes her short black hair back and forth. Selma does okay and I let her go without incident, even though I know that if the situation were real she wouldn't stand a chance. I work my way down the line, fitting my arms around the different women until I am nearly in a trance, because Diane is next and if she knows I will still have to hug her and pretend like everything is okay and I am her instructor and she is to defend herself against my imaginary advances.

"Let me go," Fran says when I won't let her out of my arms no matter how many times she kicks at my shins or tries to throw her elbow into my padded gut. I snap out of my trance and let her go and start to apologize when my words are cut short by a swinging side kick from Fran that smashes into my knee and sends me screaming to the mat.

When I don't get up, Diane is the first to break out of line and kneel beside me.

"Are you okay?" she asks.

I point at my knee, rocking, hoping the pain will go away.

"Oh, my God," Fran says, pushing Selma out of the way and kneeling beside Diane. "I'm so sorry. I'm so sorry. I thought you were ready. I thought you wanted us to defend ourselves."

"I did," I manage to croak. The pain starts to ebb a bit and I flex my knee a few times.

"Don't move it," Diane says. Her hair falls off her shoulder and pokes through the holes in my helmet. I am torn, both by my urge to prove to them that I am invincible and by my desire to let them coo and touch me for a few minutes more. Fran helps me to a sitting position and the pain in my knee flares up into my thigh before disappearing.

I pull the helmet off and rub my face and feel a hand on the back of my neck. I look up, hoping it is Diane, but instead I see Selma's smooth white arm.

"I'm okay," I say, shaking my leg for them. "See?"

"I'm so sorry, Jack," Fran says. "But . . ."

"I know," I say. "That's what they pay me the big bucks for."

Everybody laughs. I pull the suit off and limp around behind them for the rest of the class as they practice joint locks on one another. When the clock above the Peg-Board hits 8:30, I dismiss the class. They groan and shuffle toward the locker room. Just before Diane makes it to the doorway I call out to her.

"Want me to show you how to get out of a submission hold?" The words hang in the drafty gym as I limp toward her.

"How?" she asks, coming closer. I start to sweat. There are a million ways this can play out and in all of them I am the bad guy. I half expect her to tell me about the strange man outside her window, and part of me wants her to so I can nod and look concerned and maybe give her some safety tips. But she doesn't and her voice sounds flat and a little bit tired and she doesn't touch my arm when I move behind her.

"I'll show you the move," I say.

"I don't know . . ." she begins, but I cut her off.

"Like this," I say, wrapping my arms around her throat until I can feel the soft beat of her pulse against my skin and her body tense up as her hands go to her neck.

"I know," she says.

For a minute I'm not sure if she means the submission hold or if she knows that I've been looking in her windows. So I tighten my grip a little bit, and before I can ask her what she knows, she kicks my unpadded crotch. As I release her she sends two quick punches to my throat.

I go down and I feel as if I am underwater, my lungs full of ocean as the pain radiates through my stomach and up into my chest. I want to ask her what she knows, but when I roll over, she is gone and I am alone on the mats, holding myself, waiting for Mary to come in and help me to my feet.

WHAT SALMON KNOW

for DENNIS SIPE

With Marley it's all or nothing. He leads, I follow and after work that means Cheap Charlie's Klondike Bar. Knee deep in drink.

Do or die, Marley says. What's it gonna be, Craig?

I inventory the damage: six pitchers, two shots of rotgut whiskey and the brush-off from some Eskimo chick in satin hot pants. At the bar a bunch of Indians are threatening to kick the bartender's tender young hide if he don't grab them some winning pull tabs out of the bucket.

What? I shout over the jukebox.

We're going fishing, he says, leaning. Me and you and no arguments.

What about work? I say.

He gets this killer-on-the-loose look in his eyes and says, Screw it, they can't fire us, because we're hot shit good.

Then I tell him how I'm thinking about taking this tall-money gig setting truss for a new fruit-juice plant in Hawaii. It's not the job, just the getting out I'm into, but Marley's not like that. He's into loyalty and planting your feet firmly in one spot, waiting to die.

I ain't letting your country club ass leave Alaska so easy, he says. His black eyes toggle back in their sockets as he tries to flag down the waitress, who's been doing her best to avoid us.

Waitress zips up to our table and tells us the bartender won't serve us another drink, but she'd be happy to bring us some coffee or Coca-Colas. Normally Marley gets pretty fired up when he's cut off, but ten hours of slapping nails into plywood sheeting has taken the piss out of his rope. He nods and lets her bob off through the crowd, empty beer bottles in hand.

What's it gonna be? Marley says. Fish or die?

I hesitate.

Time's up, partner. I'm making an executive decision.

All I can do is nod and follow him out of the bar because Marley thinks fishing can change anything, bad luck, a sour marriage or a shitty job.

We grab our gear and white-knuckle it toward Delta. No sleep, just coffee and greasy sourdough donuts from this double-wide trailer posing as a diner.

We drive for hours until the air goes thin and cold. There are trees every which fucking way and mountains up on our right that when I remember to look at them take my breath away.

Alaska's a postcard from Hell.

Five hours later we hit the Delta Clearwater turnoff and the snow starts.

Yee-hah, Marley says, rolling the window down and letting the flakes melt around us.

We park next to the Delta Roadhouse and hike in to the river. Smoke from a late-season forest fire makes the whole place look like a battlefield as we traipse through tangled blueberry bushes, our rods out in front of us like bayonets.

Marley snaps on a Pixee, a bright silver spoon with a slit of pink down the middle. He lands four salmon in an hour, two fat hens full of eggs and a couple of bucks. We drink beer and coffee mixed together and hope to God it will do something for us.

Got one! Marley says. Now fight, you mother!

He leans back into his doubled rod and smiles. The line pulls taut and for a minute it looks as if he's getting some kind of electric current out of the water.

I know that feeling. I've gone looking for it everywhere.

Marley says he'd tear his heart through his guts to feel that first jolt of a fish on the line every day of his life.

Smoke drifts across the river. I could do with a little heat from this fire but it's mostly scrub brush and jack pine burning along the river drainage, small fire by Alaskan standards. At our last stop for gas, the cashier told us that a tribe of down-on-their-luck Tanana Indians torched some dry grass and timber hoping the state would hire them to put out the blaze.

Marley says he'd like to be a smoke jumper screaming out of the sky, attacking fires with ax and shovel. Marley's theory is that Alaska's the only place big enough for him to die in. That he needs mountains, permafrost and legions of bears to hold his soul in after he's gone. Of all the places I've run to Alaska's hooked me the deepest. One blast of seventy below zero was enough to tell me that you either had to love this place enough to die for it or else get out.

Can't feel my hands, I tell Marley.

He's got the fish on the bank, trying to run the stringer through her gill plates. She's fat with eggs and goes maybe thirteen, fourteen pounds. I watch as the rainbow of color drains out of her and she fades to a drab gray.

Shit, try two hours ago, he says. That was the last time I so much as had a tingle. He laughs and drops the fish in next to the others, where she takes out the slack and halfheartedly tries to swim upstream until the rope and the weight of the other fish on the stringer tell her it's a no-go.

How many more you want? I ask, flipping my lure out into the current. Marley wipes the blood off his gloves on the frozen grass. He's greedy about fish and likes to keep his freezer full until spring.

Until we're done, he says.

We catch two more apiece. I try and fail at building a fire. The wind gets the better of my lighter. My hands feel like bricks. Marley decides to get stoned instead.

He passes me the joint and I take a hit or two but the cold keeps the high off me.

Our lines are iced up and we've lost thirty dollars' worth of lures to snags, but Marley's still waiting to get one more fish on the line.

C'mon, I say. Let's pack it up. Drink beer and get warm.

We got to clean these fuckers first, Marley says, stabbing a finger at the stringer full of fish. Then he flips his line out into the stream again. The lure dings off a rock, before the current grabs it. I watch as it wobbles past all of the shadowy fish on their way upstream to some secret place where they can spawn, waste away and then die.

You still thinking about that Hawaii gig? Marley asks, eyes locked on his lure.

Chasing the buck, I say.

You oughta have that tattooed on your heart.

I will.

Hawaii's some soft living, he says.

They've got volcanoes, I offer.

Overrated.

Sharks? Skin cancer?

Who's dumb enough?

I give, then. You got me, I say. But I promised myself that I'd never turn down good money. I don't wanna be an old man swinging a hammer for six measly bucks an hour.

That's not what I'm sayin'. Hell, if I'm fifty and still bangin' wood I give you permission to shoot me. Euthanize my stupid ass.

It's just a job, I say.

Yeah, well, two months of that sun-and-surf bullshit and you're gonna be singing the blues. Guaran-fucking-teed.

I'll take that chance.

That's my point, Craig. There is no chance. Places like that you don't have to do a goddamn thing! The sun comes up every morning. It's always warm. You've got fruit growing on trees and tan women. You'd have to be an idiot not to get by in Hawaii!

That's what it's all about, I tell him.

Here's what it's about, he says, his voice cracking. Right here man, he says. One false move and your ass gets shit-canned. Game over. End of story. Eight million ways to die, that's what makes the living worth it!

I tell him about the twenty-five dollars an hour, only it's too late, he's already shaking his head at me like in his book I'm gonna be soft until proven otherwise.

By noon the sun's a blood-red dot behind the haze of smoke from the fire. Marley's face looks like chuck steak from the wind and beer. His dark hair hangs out of his hood in frozen clumps. I stare down at my reflection in the water and I look the same.

Marley says, How about we hump the fish out the trail and back to the roadhouse? They got a gut sink and a fire barrel. That way we won't freeze what's left of our hands gutting them out here in the water.

He pulls off his wool gloves and wriggles nine cold fingers at me. He donated the pinkie to a Skil saw earlier this year and ruined the job site's safety record after twenty-one days without so much as a splinter. Osborne Construction's got it set up so everybody on the job gets a crummy little thermos if we go thirty days without a serious injury. Fifty's a drill. Seventy-five days and everybody gets a black satin jacket with the Osborne Construction logo stitched all over the back. No job ever goes a hundred days without some fuck-up—too many drunks and dumb shits with power tools. But thirty, even fifty days, and a prize is enough to get the whole crew, even the hi-lo operators, running around acting like Christians on Good Friday.

They couldn't sew the finger back on, so Marley buried it under one of the pot plants he keeps in his backyard. Now he looks like everybody else on the job—tainted with the work. The closest I've come is a Sawzall across my forearm when some pimple-faced rookie got cocky and kept zipping through a crooked doorframe, forgetting that I was on the other side pulling shiners. The white hats had him piss-tested and fired him when it came up dirty. And I took thirty-two stitches.

Hey, Burke, you gonna watch or work?

Just watching them go upstream, I tell him. I want to argue with him some more about my leaving, but looking at the fish working in vain against the rope makes it all seem wrong. Nobody's gonna come drag me out of the water and slice my gills. I'm going to hop a plane to the Pacific and start getting soft.

Marley pauses from his task and blows on his hands, watching a column of smoke whorl across the water.

Last fish of the year, Marley says, placing a hand over his heart like he wants to pray or pledge.

Another pod of fish pulse upstream, past us. They are dying, rotting from the inside out, beaks hooked into determined snarls, hides red and scar-pocked.

Marley hauls out the first half of the stringer and saddles up his gear in his other arm. I watch as he strains to shoulder the fish. They fight him, slipping and sliding across his back, leaving a trail of mucus and blood on his fishing vest.

Sonofabitch, these things are heavy, Marley says, slogging out of the water. I wade down and grab my half and flip them over my shoulder, where they start flopping and fighting like a sack of puppies.

Normally we'd bat them dead with our fish whacker, mini Louisville sluggers with nails pounded through the barrel, but Marley forgot to bring it this time. So I walk, hoping the cold air and lack of oxygen will zap them dead.

Snowflakes come down again, the kind you can catch in your mouth and taste. I follow Marley up the trail, the stringer cutting into my palms. But for the first time in an hour I feel pain.

The trail twists out away from the river. Frozen stinkberry bushes and ferns wrapped in snowflakes line each side. I keep my eye on Marley's back full of fish, gill plates working overtime, eyes staring out at the land. I start to feel a little guilty about letting them die like this, suffocating on dry land, snow beating against their scales as the cold air stiffens their gill feathers.

Maybe we should've cut their gills back there in the water, I yell up to Marley.

He stops for a minute, shifts the fish around a little, letting them wriggle themselves out as a gust of wind snatches his hood off. He stands there, frozen hair flapping in the wind like some primitive dragging dinner back to his cave.

Fuck it, they're just fish, he says, and starts walking again.

We break out of the pines and into a short field. I can see the roadhouse ahead with a couple of trucks and Suburbans parked up against its log sides. Just as Marley stops to shift the fish around again, they give one last wriggle and one of the bucks shoots his milt out on Marley's back.

You got cum on your back, I tell him.

Fuck you, he says. He laughs and keeps walking. Two more bucks release onto his back and then the hens start dropping egg sacs that crunch under my waders.

Sonofabitch! Marley screams, dropping the fish.

He does a little dance, trying to brush the mess off his back before it freezes. I fall down in the field, laughing, and realize that the fish have been doing the same on my back. I stare up into the white swirl of the sky as the fish writhe and flop around me, releasing their sperm and roe onto the frosted ground. For a moment I'm lost in the slither and slide of the dying spawn and I think I know what Marley means.

We had it coming, he says.

I sit up, my hand mashing a puddle of roe as Marley picks an egg sac off his shoulder and flings it out into the snow. A couple of ravens swoop down off the trees and start stabbing at the eggs.

Ain't no fucking way they're going to let us in the roadhouse now, I say.

What about my truck? We've got to drive with this shit on us!

At least I'm not cold anymore, I say.

Well, getting spawned on kinda takes the cold out of you.

All around me the fish begin to stiffen, surrendering to the cold. I don't feel like laughing anymore even though I know it will make a good story for the guys on Monday.

We drag the fish the rest of the way and sling them up on a rickety table made out of scrap two-by-fours and delaminated plywood. There are a few fishermen working the water close by with buzz baits and bass rods. Hillbilly GIs, probably from one of the bases that are scattered all over nowhere in Alaska. Nobody likes them much, at least not the real Alaskans, although the governor says that military bases drive the economy and that we should welcome each new GI with open arms and smiles. I'm not keen on all that good-neighbor business. Marley feels the same, only with a vengeance because he once lost a pretty little Eskimo girl with cheekbones and one of them all-over tans to some flyboy from Fort Eielson. Because in Alaska you don't lose your women—just your turn.

I'll start gutting and you go see about getting us a few beers from the bar, I tell Marley.

Deal, he says.

And I help him brush the remainder of the eggs off his back before he slogs up to the roadhouse.

I slit the fish pee hole to gill and begin scooping out the

insides with a gut spoon. The bright red flesh feels warm and stiffens when it is exposed to the air. Overhead the ravens circle, cawing at me to toss the offal on the rocks.

Midway through the third fish one of the GIs waddles up out of the water. He's dressed head to toe in military-issue snow gear. Name stitched just above the breast pocket: GREER.

Caught you a few, he says, flashing me the army good ole boy grin.

I fling a pile of guts to the ravens before answering.

Kinda looks that way, don't it?

What did you use? he asks. He's carrying a spindly bass rod, buzz bait dangling from the end.

These ain't bass, I tell him. He frowns, adjusting a wad of chew between his cheeks. His eyes narrow and cross at me for a moment.

My buddy rigged this up for me, he says proudly, pointing at the rod.

How long you been in Alaska?

Just this spring. It's too cold for the fish to bite, not like Kentucky, where the water's like coffee.

The fish don't bite 'cause they want to eat, I tell him. They bite 'cause they're mad. Protecting their turf, you might say.

Greer's face fogs up like he's gone soft in the head from too much dry-firing down at the pistol range.

Huh?

They ain't going to bite on no bass baits. You got to use spoons or Spin 'n Glos. I say it slow.

What's a Spin 'n Glo?

Over there, I say, pointing at my tackle box.

You think maybe I could see me one of them Spin 'n Glos. 'Cause lemme tell you those are some nice fish, he says.

Go on and dig one out. They're in the bottom. Pixee's are good too.

Greer shuffles over to the box, spits a line of brown juice out onto the rocks and starts digging through my tackle. A couple of rusty hooks slice up his fingers and set him to sucking blood, but the air's cold and what hurts don't hurt for long.

Wow, this is a mess of tackle. I've got to show my buddy these things. He's a real good fisher, he says, pointing a bloody finger downriver. I nod and look back at the roadhouse waiting on Marley.

This a Spin 'n Glo?

You got it, I say.

Shit, you can't catch nothing on this. You're pulling my leg, mister. He laughs and spits some more. I catch sight of Marley, beers in hand as he walks down the slope toward the gut sink.

Howdy, Greer says. Marley shakes his head at him.

Took a little sweet talk, but I wrangled these out of the bartender, he says.

Get warm? I ask him.

And then some. Not a bad little place, he says. The bartender looks like a she-bear.

He pats his shoulder and I know he means this in a good way. Marley gives Greer one of his Billy Joe Bad-ass stares and Greer backs off a few paces.

Marley continues. Then there's this Kris Kringle–looking dude who showed me this trick with a piece of fishing line and a twenty-dollar bill. I had it figured out, but I told him I had a buddy who would fall for it hook, line and sinker.

Greer starts hopping around the gut sink.

Marley looks at him. You got a question? Problem?

You guys got a honey spot where them fish jump into your net, don't ya? Greer asks. Hell, man, I ain't caught nothing all morning except for some frostbite.

This here's the Bassmaster, I tell Marley.

Greer tries on a stupid smile.

Shit man, gimme a break, I'm from Kintucky—all's we got is bass and bluegill, he says.

Army, right? Marley asks.

Greer nods.

C'mon, tell me where you guys caught these mothers 'cause I bet they're gonna be some good eatin'. My buddy says the fillets taste just like rib eye steak.

I don't know about that, I say, handing Marley the knife and gut spoon.

Hold on a minute, Greer says. Lemme go get my buddy so you can tell him all about these Spin 'n Glos.

He flaps down to the river and starts yelling for someone named Chester.

Marley waits until Greer is far enough away from us before leaning into me.

Why didn't you just tell Jarhead to buzz off? he asks. He puts the beer can to his mouth and works it until it's half empty.

He don't mean nothing by it, I say. Just trying to catch some fish. Besides, we're the dumb motherfuckers who had fish spawn on our backs.

Marley grins. His teeth are crooked and pitted from too much coffee and cigarettes.

I'll remind you of that when we get his buddy Chester drooling all over our fish, trying to chisel a few freebies.

Pretty soon Greer comes back from the river with Chester in tow. Chester looks like a fat, sweaty desk jockey. Bowler also flashes across my mind. He's got a black NRA baseball cap shoved down low on his blotchy and swollen head.

Tell Chester about them lures you guys used, Greer says. And tell him how the fish bite 'cause they're pissed off.

Chester harrumphs and rolls his eyes around in their chubby sockets. He looks on, still panting from his walk over, as Marley cleans the last three fish.

Spin 'n Glos, I say. Greer nods and starts punching Chester in the shoulder like a kid brother.

Chester ignores him.

How exactly do you fish them? Chester asks.

Leader and then the sinker, I say. About twelve inches, depends on how deep you wanna fish.

What about the spoons? he says.

You stick 'em up your ass and jerk real hard, Marley says.

Chester looks at him and says, I'll let that one go.

Then Greer whispers something to Chester. They laugh.

Leapfrog, Greer says.

Chester bugs his eyes and sticks his tongue out.

Ribbit! he says.

Both of them fall out giggling. Marley and I stare at their private joke. I hold back the urge to ask what the fuck they're talking about.

Take 'em, Marley says, pointing at the lures.

Of course not—we'll buy them, Chester says, looking all smart and superior. Greer nods and fixes his hair up under his hood.

Just go ahead and take them, I say, wanting to get rid of Chester and Greer.

They mean it, Chester, Greer says, still smiling from their little joke. Chester rolls his eyes, his tongue lapping at his bacon-colored lips as he considers our offer.

You really caught those with these? Chester asks.

Marley and I nod.

Well, then I suppose we might borrow a few. Try our luck. Cast about, Chester says. As long as it's no trouble.

Ask them about their honey spot, Chester, go on and ask 'em. I bet the fish are thick as flies, Greer says, circling his buddy, stupid lapdog grin frozen to his face.

Chester ignores him and goes over to the tackle box, where he pulls out two Pixees and three Spin 'n Glos.

Gentlemen, Chester says, sucking in his gut. Gentlemen, we thank you for your wisdom and generosity.

He puts his hand over his heart for a minute as if to bless us. Something in Chester's voice moves Greer to snatch off his hood and look skyward.

Marley just stands there shaking his head.

Catch 'em, I say, trying not to laugh. Catch 'em good.

Chester and Greer salute, before heading back to the river, Greer orbiting around Chester's bulk, stopping every once in a while to slap him on the back or muss his hat.

Was that shit for real? Marley asks.

They get guns and get to ride around in tanks, I say.

Good fucking riddance, Marley says. I need a beer. You buying?

As long as you don't start on that Hawaii crap.

Scout's honor, I say.

We do the roadhouse, play Moe Bandy on the jukebox, roll dice for drinks. I fall for the twenty-dollar-bill trick, bump my head chasing after it, giving the gray hair a good laugh. The bartender does sort of look like a bear, but she has a nice smile and after a couple of beers I'm flirting with her. Her name is Sherise and she lets me feel the muscles in her shoulders.

Chopping wood, she says. Does wonders for the body.

Marley starts humming the theme from *Hawaii Five-O* and calls me a soft sonofabitch.

Just then Greer comes bobbing into the bar and slaps us on the back.

We're getting 'em, he says. You gotta come see the one Chester's got on now!

Marley peels Greer's hand off his shoulder.

We're just about ready to hit the road, I say.

Come on, guys, you've got to see Chester.

We don't wanna see Chester, Marley says.

We're getting 'em now. Chester's got one twice as big as any of those minnows you peckerwoods were cleaning.

He spreads his arms to show us how big.

Peckerwoods, eh? Marley asks.

I realize that Greer's both stupid and drunk.

Shit, man, I was kidding about that peckerwood stuff, Greer says. Just come see the fish!

How big? Marley asks, invading Greer's personal space. I can see that the thought of some dumb-ass GI catching a big fish on his lures burns Marley up.

Might as well. Then we've gotta hit the road, I say.

Greer lights up with a pumpkin grin, dashes out of the bar, heading toward the river.

We follow. After the bar and beer the cold isn't so bad. But then I see the river, sun bouncing off its icy water, mountains in the distance tall and silent, like ghosts. Perfect, until I see Greer splashing into the shallows like some kind of retarded cheerleader and then Chester standing on the bank, leaning over his bent rod. The line vibrates and hums as the fish pulls into it.

Marley grabs me and points. You gonna leave Alaska to idiots like this? he asks.

Chester turns, his face red with exertion. It's Moby fucking Dick, he grunts.

The fish breaks water and it's so big both of us just stop for a moment to admire the slab of its massive back and the sing of taut line as it makes another run.

Let it run and try and beach it, Marley says.

Chester nods and goes back to his task, taking in line when the fish gives it to him, obeying the current.

Pull, Chester, pull, Greer screams.

The fish breaks water again, trying to shake the lure free. Then it makes a run at us as Chester dashes up on shore, chest heaving with exertion, cranking in line.

That's it—ease it in, Marley says. Ease it in.

Pull back, I say.

Chester pulls and pulls on the rod until the confused fish skitters into the shallows. Greer runs behind it and kicks it up onto shore like a soccer ball.

The fish wriggles against the rocks; its gills billowing in and out with the strange air it's getting. Chester falls back on a large rock and clutches at his chest.

You got her! Greer yells. Look at the size of that mother! It's a goddamn fuckin' monster.

Shut up and get the fillets, Chester wheezes, throwing his knife at Greer.

Beat it with a rock first, I say.

But Greer just shakes his head, picks up the knife and jumps on the fish. The fish makes gurgling noises and Marley looks at me.

What the fuck are they doing? he asks me.

I watch as Chester gets to his knees, his face wet with sweat. Sand and small pebbles are stuck to his cheek, like tears. Marley starts to say something but stops when Greer plunges the knife into the shoulder of the fish and runs the blade back toward the tail. The fish squirms and wriggles, blood shooting everywhere as a long red fillet slides off the fish. Greer quickly does the same thing on the other side of the stunned fish. He holds up the two slabs of red flesh which seem to quiver and shake as if they are alive. Beneath him, the fish snakes around the rocks, sideless and bleeding like hell. Chester stands and picks the lure out of the salmon's jaw. I move up closer as Greer does a little jig with the meat in his hands and Chester kicks the fish back into the river. It rests for a minute, confused by its missing meat, before trying to swim upstream.

Marley stands next to me, fist pumping open and shut.

I'll be damned, Chester says. You missed some of that tail meat. He points at the fish, which is still struggling upstream to spawn.

Kill the fucking fish, Marley says. Kill the fish or I'm gonna fillet your fucking ass! He balls his fists. I move down closer to the water and watch as a couple of other salmon swim behind their scalped brother.

It'll die, Chester says.

Bullshit, I say. Not till it spawns.

Chester looks confused. Greer stops his fish jig, the fillets hanging at his sides like broken wings.

So it spawns. What's it matter to you? Chester says.

I watch as the fish scoots a little further out into the stream, somehow finding a way to right itself despite its wounds.

Then Marley pushes Greer into the stream.

Go on. Kill it or I start stomping some army ass, Marley says.

Greer looks at Chester for help.

Kill the fish, put it out of its misery, Marley says again. He's calmer now, maybe a little drunk and he eyes me as I begin wading out further into the current.

Not you, Marley says.

Tell your buddy to back off, Chester says.

I shrug my shoulders and lean out into the water to look at the fish swimming in its own cloud of blood. I can see its heart beating under the skin, pounding and thumping like it's never going to quit.

I stand there a moment, staring up into the sky. I turn to Marley, his eyes are peeled back like eggs, fists ready to go. Hawaii seems small now, a soft brown dot on the map surrounded by blue, full of easygoing islanders who dress in flowered shirts and say things like "Hang loose" and "Check the waves." Part of me wants to dig in and draw a line in the sand, like Marley. Spit in the wind and pick fights I might lose—defend Alaska from Greer and Chester. I want to know what the salmon know when they're blasting upstream to die.

Marley pushes Greer further out into the water until he's standing next to me.

Halt, Chester says. He crouches his chubby body and raises his fists. His eyes go down to slits as he does a little kung-fu exhale.

Marley looks back at him and says, Shut the fuck up!

But Chester advances, hissing and snapping his fists in the air.

Marley picks up rocks and loads his fists around them. He lines up on Chester. In front of me Greer moves out toward the fish, his hands working under the cold water like steel traps while I pray deep down in my heart of hearts that the fish manages to slip away and let the stream do the killing and not some stupid, red-faced GI.

Marley swings at Chester, who takes the shot in the gut and answers with a clumsy bear hug. They fall down on the bank, tumbling over each other, Chester hissing and grunting, Marley swinging away at his head with rocks in his fists.

I freeze up and let the current pass through my legs. Salmon bump against me on their way upstream. Greer chases after the bloody fish as it swims on its side, one eye looking up at something, the other searching the gravel river bottom for its spawning ground. And me? I could stay out here forever, watching, waiting for something better to come along and pull me one way or another. But there is Marley, rocks in fist, his face speckled with Chester's blood. And the fish, snaking away from us all, too stupid to know when to quit and die.

ALL THAT GOOD STUFF

"I hope it falls off," was the last thing Mary said before she left.

She was pointing at my crotch.

She'd caught me lying about Delilah, this big blonde honey I was having some fun with. Said she could smell her on me. And she was right. Delilah wore a lot of perfume because she worked with dead people all day, styling their hair and doing makeup at Davis Funeral Home.

I didn't love Delilah. But Mary wanted answers and all I could do was stand there as my balls shriveled up into my stomach where she'd touched me. Then she did one of those Joan Crawford turns and walked out the door.

Weeks went by. I began thinking about Mary. The way her feet felt when she walked on my sore back. And how she was good at the little things, like Denver omelets and keeping the checkbook balanced. Or the way her hair smelled when she stepped out of the shower and asked me to towel her off. The problem was that I'd had it too good. She deserved better and I knew that.

No Mary and I was a mess, sitting around the house eating canned chili and staring at the bikini-skinned women of *Baywatch*. I tried masturbation and failed. Mary called once to ask if it had fallen off yet. I started to say something but then she hung up—ruined *Baywatch* for me and I had to start all over with those women on CNN.

When the divorce papers came through and I heard from a mutual friend that Mary had finally left town, I started drinking. I sold my truck and bought a late-model Buick with tinted windows and chrome rims. I wore sunglasses and a baseball hat pulled down low over my eyes. I was aiming for melancholy, but there wasn't enough rain that year to do it up right, so I settled for self-pity with some mood swing dappled in for dramatic effect. After work, feeling only slightly suicidal, I stumbled down to the softball field just to be around people.

There were plenty of teams around, guys mostly, some women. There was even a team made up of divorced women, who called themselves the Hellcats and were sponsored by MacNeil's Dairy Queen. They did a lot of snarling. There was this team of lesbians I liked to watch. They could hit and throw and I envied the way they went about the game—as if it really meant something to be out on that field, under the bright lights.

One time I watched their second baseman scrape up her knee sliding into third. All of the women gathered around and helped her to the bench, mussed her hair and told her she'd be all right as she limped and tried to put a game face on the situation. Then one of the women looked up into the stands and glared at me. I had my sunglasses on, a pint of whiskey in my pocket—a spy in the house of sisterly love.

They sent their tank of a first baseman over to ask me what I was doing. She had big round shoulders and a Pete Rose bowl cut.

"The men's league is over there," she said, pointing at a group of potbellied men screaming and yelling for pop-ups.

"I like to watch you guys," I said.

She blushed and I tipped my sunglasses at her and after a few minutes she shuffled back to her teammates, reporting that I was just some harmless drunk and that if I caused any problems she could "take care of me."

All around me it seemed that men were falling to pieces, stabbing at foolish things like the Foreign Legion, tattoos, Harleys, eighteen-year-old girlfriends, hair weaves, bicycle shorts in public, skydiving classes and massive amounts of midlife drinking and drugs.

I sought help directly.

Help came from A Man's Forum: Counseling and Crisis Center, presided over by Dr. John with eloquence, austerity and good old common sense. Dr. John was a tall man with a salt-and-pepper beard, a face like an old mitt left out in the rain. Oh, and he had the eyes—great blue beamers that could ferret out your deepest secrets. He was fond of saying things like "Trust yourself" and "Manhood is not a brotherhood, it's understood."

There were others like me. Guys with all sorts of shortcomings and problems—anger, booze, drugs, sexual problems and deviancy, etc.

"It's all quite normal," Dr. John said during our first session. I stared at the thick door and the fifty-minute clock sitting on his desk. "There are terms for what you're experiencing, Chester. Event-induced impotency. Temporary, I assure you."

"Just give me the Viagra and let's be done with it."

His eyelids fell to half-mast. "Very interesting. Do you have somebody in mind?"

I looked at him.

"The Viagra," he said, straightening his index finger in the air. "Do you have a target audience?"

I hesitated.

"Well," he said, tapping his head, "I can assure you that your problems are all up here. I'm afraid a mountain of the stuff would do you no good."

"But Mary put some kind of curse on it," I said.

He shook his head. "Have you tried masturbating? Fantasizing?"

I told him about Mary's curse and my failed attempts at masturbation.

"Far more troubling is your use of alcohol," he said. "This curse you say your wife has put on you, it makes you want to drink, no?"

I nodded, wanting to believe that all this was some temporary funk or middle-aged rut that would run its course and leave me with enough time to contemplate death. So I talked, unbuckling long complicated filibusters about my past—perceived slights, certain manly injustices I'd suffered on the way. And he listened, goading me on with grandfatherly nods and those eyes. He loaned me books on impotency and substance abuse, sent me to seminars where whole roomfuls of fellow limp dicks squirmed and listened while some white-haired doctor told us to buck up and begin to see ourselves as whole beings. They taught us to visualize—sunsets or mountains at first, then they stepped on the gas and told us to see naked women, imagine their skin, the smell. So I closed my eyes and tried to imagine ex-wife Mary. When that didn't work, I tried Delilah, but then I started thinking about dead people.

HOW IT BEGAN

We called our softball team the Dys-Functionals and we came together in the waiting room. Dr. John knows that men won't normally strike up a conversation (except in hardware stores and parking lots). As he sees it, men have to be coerced. Put us in a large room with plenty of corners and an ample supply of *Sports Illustrated* and forget the conversation.

Not Dr. John.

He cramped us with small tables and chairs, one coffeepot and only two magazines, *Highlights* and *Good Housekeeping*. He told us that we were a family of sorts and that we should reach out to one another. Gradually we started to talk. A few of us at first. I met Max, Stilton and Lanny on my third visit. Max was full of words—gay, I thought, or at least latent, the woman in him crawling out like a rash. Stilton, who said he had multiple eating disorders, panted too much and emitted a pungent eau-de-fat-guy aroma. And Lanny, well he was overly friendly, giggled a lot and drank coffee like it was Budweiser. They in turn met others and so on and so on.

WHAT WE FOUND OUT

We liked balls. Balls of any kind and sports. Most of us had slid clammy, five-fingered gloves over our hands and stared into the sun waiting for a baseball to descend. The very idea of taking a field united, together, as a team seemed a remote and distant possibility.

I told the guys about how the lesbians looked after one another, how they faced up to the disapproving stares of old folks and teenagers when they walked hand in hand down the gravel path to take practice.

"They were a team," I said. "They helped each other out."

Lanny suggested we get together, toss a ball around and see what would happen. Then Stilton hung a flyer in the office announcing the formation of a softball team and before I knew it I was out on a field shagging grounders.

For the most part we were athletic flunkies. But the idea of fielding a team wouldn't die. All of us loved the good game—the tobacco, pine tar, beer, pretty divorced women in the stands, hot dogs, dirt, straight white-powdered lines and home plate. Most of all, we loved the idea of hitting the ball, striking it high into the air or making it sing on a wicked grounder.

Then there was the warrior thing. The awful urge to stretch hamstrings, skin knuckles, bang knees. Our sagging middle-aged bodies yearned to be out on the grass, under the lights, swinging away at some perfect piece of our childhood. We were hackers, but we managed to come together, ten mixed-up men with bats, balls, gloves and dreams—a team.

WHO'S ON FIRST

Stilton occupied first like the Imperial German Army—big, brassy and fat. He sprawled at first base, glove in hand, his pockets full of snack-sized Snickers and M&M's. At the plate he was a monster, singularly bent on crushing every ball that floated his way. By his own admission, he had the suppressed-anger thing going pretty good, clogged arteries and a foul mouth.

Binx played shortstop. He wore his hat high and queer like Larry Bowa. As for his fielding abilities, he was solid, but dysfunctional as hell, and like me a limp dick. Stage fright. No Viagra for him. He was twice divorced from a pair of scary fat women whom he still loved and went shopping with on alternating weekends.

If there was true talent on our team, Janitor Bill, our

third baseman, possessed it. There was grace in the way he shuffled for a one-hopper, dove at liners and always seemed to come up with that one big hit. Otherwise, he was a despicable ex-con who entertained paranoid thoughts that the world would one day be run by midgets and Freemasons. To this end he claimed to be a senior editor at an underground newsletter called the *High Lonesome,* which was dedicated to discrediting the Freemasons.

The outfield consisted of Maynard, Maynard and Maynard. Triplets and drug addicts. Steve sniffed glue, Grant cocaine and Pete preferred the old in-out with a needle, shooting up anything he could get his hands on. They held their own, though, shagging down routine fly balls and outlegging any hit that aspired to homerdom. The problem was that the brothers were never clean at the same time and we had to endure a rotational sort of Zen in our outfield.

For short fielder, Stilton recruited his manic-depressive buddy, Bob Fleeber. Fleebs wore dark socks and tinted glasses all the time and spoke in rapid gunshot bursts as if the words tasted bad in his mouth. He had self-esteem problems and hated his mother.

Max pitched. He took my story about watching the lesbians and ran with it all the way down to city hall, where he registered us for the fall softball league.

My teammates called me Lilly, but my real name is Rose, Chester B. Rose—B for Branford. I played second with a mixture of choke and grace: simple grounders confounded me, slipped out to pasture, allowing any two-bit rumdog on base to score. But give me a looper or a bouncing Betty and I'd snag it, turning and throwing the ball like an

All-Star. The more difficult, the better. Dr. John had a fancy name for my ability to flub the most mundane catches, just like he called me impotent, with the fifty-minute clock ticking.

In session, after noticing my predilection for choke.

"Given time to fail, the inner child recalls in a split second every past failure, thus inducing a like reaction—the will to commit failure. That, Chester, is your burden. The cross I must help you carry and eventually shrug off."

"You're right, Doc. Oh, yes, right as rain and all that," I said, hoping we'd move on to some small detail that would allow me to squirm and stall my way through the last of the session.

"Failure is very important to you, isn't it? We must examine why—perhaps this is why you feel the urge to drink."

"Ten days," I said, holding out my hands to show him how they were shaking.

"But the need is still there, no?"

I nodded and slouched deeper into the chair.

WHERE WE WERE

Each game was played under the lights at Caller Cutter Softball Park—called it CC, like the whiskey—and before each game we would meet in the parking lot, smoke cigarettes and drink coffee out of thermoses while the other teams knocked back beers and blasted classic rock on shitty car speakers.

But it was the sight of the field on a Saturday night that we lived for—the lights, kids playing tag in abandoned dugouts, the smell of river water and fresh-cut grass and the sharp ping of aluminum bats.

There was a royal blue concession stand nestled at the park's entrance. The words CANDY and POP written in large red letters. Helga, a rough-voiced woman with oil-black eyes and the sort of blonde hair that you couldn't help but look at ran the stand with a haughty elegance that made me feel unworthy every time I ordered a Coke and hot dog. Her slight German accent didn't help matters much.

"You vant?" she'd say, fixing her eyes on me, dragging on her cigarette as if she was in some sort of movie. Binx claimed she was a man-eater and would run away to his car every time he saw her coming down the worn dirt path, her arms full of buns and boxes of Good and Plenty candy.

It was customary to check in on Helga, buy a Popsicle or Coke, and flirt with her or at least approximate flirting.

More than once I winked and smiled at her as she made change and pushed the mustard bottle across the counter at me.

"Come here," she said, curling her finger at me.

I trotted around to the back of the stand where dark pools of old soda syrup stained the dirt like blood and the air smelled of hot garbage.

"I can be a real pain, mister. You start vinking and who knows vat could happen," Helga said.

I said some moonbeam thing or another and waited for a sign. Instead she frowned at me.

"You're not ready for the big leagues yet," she said.

"Oh, yeah," I said.

She squared her shoulders. "It's vritten all over you," she said, pulling a cigarette out of her pocket.

"What's that?"

"Vhen you're ready to play you come back and talk to Helga," she said, slamming the door in my face.

THE SEASON

In our first game, against Rathman's Pipe & Supply, it became glaringly obvious that we were not bound for glory. Stilton ate too many hot dogs and proceeded to hurl the contents of his many-chambered stomach against the dugout wall.

Max tried to rattle Rathman with his spastic banter that seemed to spill out of his mouth. "Hey, batter, batter, batter, splatter, fatter, ratter, hatter, shitter, shatter."

"Shut up, you fucking homo," Janitor Bill threatened, a wad of tobacco bulging in his right cheek. Max considered the fact that he might be a homosexual and became withdrawn. I had a vision of ex-wife Mary leaning her hips into me and biting my nipple. The vision broke, and I was still in the dugout feeling sick and hungover. The triplets sat knee to knee to knee, chewing gum, whispering among themselves. Steve looked gone, his eyes like marbles, skin the color of milk. I could smell model glue on his breath. Dr. John paced the dugout and watched as the Pipers flung the ball back and forth to each other and smacked their mitts. He looked worried, concerned for his crew of psychos and misfits because win or lose it was his job to keep us together.

The rest of us looked at the Pipers, searching for that chink in the armor, contemptuous of their seemingly normal jocularity or the way they tossed the ball, confident of each catch. These were real men, men with wives and happy well-adjusted children. We prided ourselves on our ability to single out the weak or deviant on the opposing team.

"Look at Mr. Mustache on third," Binx said. He poked me in the ribs more than was necessary to get my attention. I eyed a potbellied man with powerful arms and tattoos.

"Yeah, what about him?"

"He's got problems," Binx said. "Big problems."

Meanwhile, Hornets had discovered Stilton's gift and were buzzing around the dugout, causing Janitor Bill to scream and swing at the air every time one of them flew near.

"How do you know?" I said.

"See the way he chews down on his mustache? That's a sign of tension," Binx said, hustling his balls back and forth a few too many times.

"Looks pretty normal to me." In fact the guy looked like he could bend pipe with his bare hands.

"Naw, look deeper, under all that regular meat-and-potatoes-guy crap."

"He looks like he wants to kick our asses," I said.

"He beats his wife," Binx said. "That's it—that's his problem—all that macho and no place for it to go." I thought about Binx then, lying spraddle-legged in bed, his wife/girlfriend upset, penis limp, his face a knot of concentration and anger. I sympathized. He had the right to suspect that there were other, seemingly normal men out there who deep down were just as broken and scared.

In the corner, Stilton looked better, a few hot dogs lighter, color marching back to his face. The triplets were up swinging bats. Dr. John paced. Janitor Bill swung his hands at the remaining hornets and I pounded my mitt.

We were on our way.

We took our chops. Stilton, Binx and Lanny went down swinging. Dr. John clapped, "Go get 'em boys, chins up." We took the field and watched our dreams smacked skyward as the Pipers piled on the runs, shooting balls through our legs and sailing over our heads. Stilton barfed again and Binx kept up his nervous chatter. Finally, the triplets managed to pull a few of the balls out of the air to end the inning. Dr. John paced the dugout dispensing mini counseling nuggets in a vain attempt to hold his team together. But it was too late.

We lost, managing only a few hits and not many outs. I went hitless. Then all hell broke loose. Janitor Bill threw a rock at their pitcher. Max tried to grab the first baseman's ass. Binx asked Mr. Mustache if he got off on hitting women and received a black eye in return.

Afterward, our bright uniforms smudged with dirt and lime, we sat knock-kneed and silent, in the dugout as Dr. John strode before us like Ahab, jaw tight, eyes scanning the lot of us for that great white whale of our lost egos. This was a man who bought cars, paid his bills and took his wife out to nice restaurants with our money. Dirty money, fifty-minute-clock money. Our screwed-up lives had made this man wealthy.

"Two hands, men. It takes two hands some days to find that ego of ours, but it's there. Let me tell you it's there. Today, we went up against the tower of our past defeats, and we faced them, looked them square in the eye and said, Come and get us. We did, however, lose. But that is not what went on out there on that diamond today," Dr. John said.

"What went on, then?" Lanny said, his eyes rimmed with tears.

"Magnificence went on."

"Magnificence?" Stilton asked.

"Bullshit," Janitor Bill barked. "That's what went on. We got our asses kicked."

"Bill's right," Fleebs said. "We sucked pond water."

Bill glared at Fleebs. "Shut up, you dark-sock-wearing motherfucker, unless you want a lifetime subscription to pain and misery."

Fleebs started shaking.

Dr. John placed a fatherly hand on Janitor Bill and whispered something in his ear that made him whimper and look down between his legs at the dirt. Then Dr. John spread his hands wide as if in benediction and continued.

"Yes, a grand day. I'm a damn proud physician. In two days we go up against Jeeter's Auto Body, and I say we strap it on, lace it up and go back out there and play to win." Dr. John half expected us to cheer, or at least to stand up and straighten our hangdog heads. We did nothing, as the thought of another game seeped through our heads like winter under a door.

We watched as the last of the Pipers hugged his wife, patted his blonde children on the head and swung his bat over his shoulder. A Kodak moment. Binx gave the man the finger and I helped two of the triplets carry their fallen brother to the car.

When I returned to the field Max was waiting for me.

"Lily," he said.

"Rose," I corrected. He laughed, slapped his arm around me.

"Whatever. You wanna get a beer?"

I saw the tumblers of Wild Turkey, ashtrays heaped with butts and tried to wash the thought away and decided to be miserable. I didn't want to set any precedents or after-game routines that I would more than likely screw up in the long run.

"No, thanks, Max."

"Fuck you, Lily."

"Rose," I corrected as he stalked off. If I could have been with anybody, any cracked heart from our team, it would have been Stilton. Real punishment there—watching him dive into plates of postgame pasta, drinking rivers of milk and inhaling flats of sheet cake as if they were crackers.

On the way out I passed the concession stand and stopped for a Coke. Helga, who had been fiddling with the pop machine, looked at me and said, "Hey, big leaguer, you look like you need some loving."

A pimple-faced teenager who had been standing at the condiment rack looked at us and blushed.

Helga flashed me the eyes and I got scared and ran to my car.

We flailed, chopped and bungled our way through thirteen straight losses. A disgrace in anybody's book. I even ran into one of the lesbians and asked her for a few pointers on hitting.

"Visualize that you're hitting the ball," she said. Her powerful shoulders rippled as she swung a bat for me. I tried a few.

"No," she said. "Like this."

Then she stood behind me and wrapped me in her arms. She smelled like mud and straw flowers. I could feel the muscles in her chest rolling across my back. It was good.

At the end of each game we slumped and whined as Dr. John tried to do what an army of Freuds and Rocknes couldn't. We were losers, and as the last game drew near with Rexall Drugs, we had already surrendered our souls to the almighty loss column. There was a certain gutter-bound purity in losing every game—being hit, pitched and ground into oblivion.

Things veered from bad to worse. Stilton had gained thirty pounds, Janitor Bill had been arrested twice for assault in the parking lot, Binx couldn't stop muttering to himself, Max became withdrawn and sometimes refused to walk out to the mound, the triplets had lost control of their systematic abuse and began showing up at games high in pairs or sometimes not at all. Lanny quit and was quickly replaced by Mars, a pink-faced bed wetter who couldn't catch a cold, much less the floaters tossed by Max.

And I slept with Helga.

HELGA

It happened at Digger's, a clubby, vinyl-encrusted sports bar. I was watching Roger Clemens smoke 'em down on the tube, his thick shoulders and hawk eyes scaring the batters away from the plate. And after six whiskeys I'd convinced myself that baby-faced Roger was the quintessential man, a fastball-whippin' length of testosterone. Then I did the math—divided me into him and came up with a negative sum. I was unfit to carry the jock of the man who carried his jock. That was until Helga sidled up in a wrinkled white blouse, a Pall Mall dangling out of her full lips, whiskey on her breath. I nodded, sipped my drink and tried to suck in my gut.

"Hey, Fastball, you going to have a drink with me?" she asked, giving me this Marlene Dietrich leer.

My hands started shaking and I suddenly felt smart and charming.

I asked her if she wanted to go for a ride.

"Maybe you buy me a drink first. Then I go with you," she said.

I pulled out my money and set it on the drink rail in front of her.

"That's better," she said. "I like a man who listens."

After we'd run through the cash she led me back to her trailer. It was a miserable little shoe box set on a cracked concrete slab. The inside was neat, full of cut flowers and candles. She put on some Patsy Cline and I told her all about Mary.

"Dahling," she said. "Stop acting like a wanker and pour us more drinks."

I poured.

We got naked and nothing happened. I watched her light a cigarette and blow the smoke out of her nostrils.

We kissed some more. Still nothing. She pushed me back on the bed and straddled me. I closed my eyes and tried to visualize Mary somehow.

"What do you see?" she asked.

I lied and said nothing.

"This wife," Helga said. "She fucked with your head, no? Did she take your pathetic little friend with her?" She pointed at my penis.

I shook my head no and started to tell her how I was the bad guy.

She put a finger to my lips. "Enough talking," she said. "You're making me think I should stick with married men."

"Why?" I asked.

"Balls," she said. "Now be quiet while I think."

She paused to light another cigarette and then began barking out orders.

I followed—rolling around, licking, sucking and pawing at her with an alcoholic fury that would later make Dr. John blush in session.

"Much better," she said, after we had finished. "You'll come around."

Then she laughed and rolled off the bed.

We kept at this for three weeks, the twilight of our season. Once or twice a week she'd show up at my door with a bottle wrapped in a brown sack, arch her neatly plucked eyebrows and push past me to the kitchen, where she would start pouring. She said I was her project, that I needed to feel dirty and used before we could make love.

We tried. She would berate me for my impotence. She even bit me after we'd been rolling around the better part of an hour.

Still, I can't say that I wasn't stirred—moved in a certain direction with Helga. I had a mental erection of sorts when I looked in the mirror and realized that I'd become a bad person's plaything and wanted out.

THE LAST GAME

On the way to our last game Helga passed out in my lap. We had been at a bar all afternoon playing pool, drinking doubles, sucking lime wedges and grazing on beer nuts. When I pulled into the parking lot I felt something quit in me. I left Helga sleeping in my car with a note pinned to her shirt:

> *Helga,*
>
> *I am a sick man . . . I am a spiteful man, but most of all I*

need my space. Etc., etc. Your secrets are safe with me.

All that good stuff,
Chester

Rexall Drugs looked every bit as good as the last team. They swung, caught and ran with purpose. Needless to say, there was fear among my fellow Dys-Functionals. Coach John sat at the end of the bench with his hat pulled low. The ump clapped, whistled and then cleared the field. The lights came up. The sun set. Rexall took the field, and we swung at the white ball that seemed to hang forever in the dying light. Janitor Bill went down first, a grounder to second, the out smacking the first baseman's mitt like a gunshot. Mars followed and Stilton next with a long shot to left that looked golden to us before it landed gently in the fielder's glove.

We took the field. The triplets did their level best to stumble out into the green and take up their positions. Grant looked coked to the gills. Binx stomped at short, bent low like a pro and started his chatter, stopping every syllable or so to rearrange his nuts against his leg and shift his dick. Fleebs began kicking dirt across the infield, talking to himself. Max lofted the pitches and Rexall sent them flying.

But after six innings we were somehow even. Stilton had managed a home run, Pete a single and Janitor Bill two triples to score. There was even talk of victory on the bench as we squinted out into the glare of the lights.

We took the field in the top of the seventh and nobody

said a word. Rexall looked worried. A rotten-faced bum had moved behind the backstop and was taunting Rexall with every swing. Stilton said the bum looked a little like Lanny. I checked over my shoulder at Grant in the outfield, who seemed better and nearly sober. The other two triplets pounded their gloves in unison, pacing the grass.

After a leadoff homer by this barrel-chested outfielder we put them down one-two-three and hit the dugout at full sprint. When we stared at the scoreboard none of it seemed to matter. We were down one run and nobody could take that away from us.

Binx sapped a weak hopper between the third baseman's knees that slipped into the outfield. Suddenly the tying run was on first. The bum roared and rattled the chain-link backstop like a caged gorilla. Stilton yelled out Lanny's name and the bum stopped and gave us a thumbs-up. Dr. John just shook his head as Lanny got down on his knees and clasped his hands.

"The crazy bastard is praying for us," Janitor Bill snarled.

"I think he's drunk," Mars said.

"Oh really," Janitor Bill said, glaring at Mars.

On the field Max took the plate and smacked a double. Binx tripped on second base and had to hold up at third. The entire Rexall team huddled around the pitcher. Now the winning run was a hit away. Lanny stumbled up out of the dirt and put his hand on his heart and began to recite the "Pledge of Allegiance" until one of the Rexall players' wives pegged him with an empty beer can and sent him sprawling to the dirt. Janitor Bill leaped off the bench and was ready to tear-ass across the field to defend his ex-teammate, but Dr. John put a stop to it with a little time-out chat.

"Let's win one for him," Dr. John shouted.

"Win one for Lanny?" I asked.

"It's the least we can do," Dr. John said solemnly.

The triplets began tapping their bats against the bench as Rexall broke their huddle and Mars stepped off the warm-up circle to the plate. The wives and children in the bleachers rattled themselves into a hush. Mars dribbled one to first base and got tagged out. Janitor Bill whiffed and I stepped up to the plate.

Nobody said a word. Dr. John lifted his eyebrows at me as I stepped into the box and took a strike.

I ran the count full on another foul and a couple of nasty arcs from the pitcher. I started thinking about Helga and then Mary as I looked up into the lights, waiting on the pitch. The pitcher wound, the infielders took their last shuffles in the dirt and Max stepped off second a few paces. The ball rose and fell. I swung, felt the pull of ball and bat and took off running. The ball, however, plopped down soundly into the short fielder's glove. There was a moment of breathless silence and then one of the kids began shrieking from the bleachers. The pitcher stopped and all eyes turned to left field. I saw Helga.

She was naked and I could tell she was out-of-her-mind drunk by the way her body listed from side to side.

Rexall stopped, all ten men frozen in mid-shift to watch Helga. People in the bleachers started stomping their feet in unison. Dr. John eagle-eyed me. Stilton made as if he was going to puke, and for a minute Binx stopped playing with his balls on third and stared at me like Jesus on the cross.

When she hit second the crowd went nuts and began tossing things out onto the field. Max fell to the dirt and began crying; the second baseman squatted to comfort him. His season was over and now this—a naked woman walking across his field of dreams.

Janitor Bill came out of the dugout to get a better look. Mars wet himself.

"Jesus fucking Christ," Max said. Helga hit home. There were tears on her cheeks, long ribbons of wetness that pooled out of her black eyes.

I was a man with no past or present. I'd failed to win the game for us, flunked Mary and now I'd gone and quit Helga.

But there was Helga sobbing, "Dahling, dahling. Vhy do you hurt me?" My crumpled note clenched in her fist.

Lanny ran out onto the field and began running the bases, his arms raised above his head like Bruce Jenner, basking in the cheer of the crowd.

And me?

I looked up at the scoreboard, then back to Helga. Somebody was rushing at her with a coat to cover her nakedness. I could hear music coming from somewhere in the distance, and when I turned to face it, it was gone.

I looked at Helga again. Then she hugged me. I was on a baseball field, drunk, my arms wrapped around a woman I didn't love, and it all seemed so perfect—so good that it should come down to this.

DRYFALL

There was, in our family, a slow turning away from the facts of our lives. For years our father went around with other women, drank too much and fought, and generally gave the family name a rough going-over until they caught him kiting checks at a Kmart in Cleveland. My father was not a nice man, but Mother would hear none of it. Instead, she chose to ignore his run-ins with the law or the women tossing gin bottles through our windows when my father had drunk up all his money and most of the unlucky woman's. After a while I suppose the lies my mother told herself didn't matter so much. They kept her going, always looking around the corner for something good to happen. And when our father finally ran off for good it was as if he'd never existed. She put his clothes out on the curb, wrapped his shoes in garbage bags and had us cart his books over to the Salvation Army. When we returned the house had been cleaned, the walls washed with Murphy's Oil soap and the wood floors with vinegar and water. Then she sent my older brother Larry to the store for a bottle of wine. During dinner she gave us each a half glass of the wine and toasted our father, telling us that wherever he was it was better than here. I could see she wanted to cry, but then Larry asked her if it was okay to drink the wine.

"You're the man of the house now," she said.

Larry smiled, sipped the wine and then made a face.

"Nothing's ever how you think it's going to be," she said. Then she took the rest of the wine into her room and left us to do the dishes. I could hear the radio playing softly through the locked door. She was singing along to bits and pieces of song.

He never came back.

Mother worked two jobs and saw us through high school before she took up with a man named Vinny Fanshawe, who stripped cars for a living and wore dentures that didn't fit him. But she said she liked his deliberate walk, and the way he talked with his hands reminded her of a man on television. Vinny had little tolerance for Larry and me. He kept to himself, preferring instead the basement, where he could drink his vodka out of a coffee mug and pretend to build birdhouses. He said they were for starlings and when I asked him what a starling looked like he grumbled and told me to go look it up.

He never finished a single birdhouse and eventually went blind from diabetes. His drinking worsened until his kidneys hemorrhaged and we found him dead next to his workbench. A half-built A-frame birdhouse and an empty Smirnoff bottle were the only evidence left to remind us that a man other than our father had ever lived in the house. After that Larry left home and went out West, where he followed the wheat harvest from town to town, sometimes ending up in Canada, where he said the people asked you right into their homes and fed you dinner.

I stayed around town, drove a delivery truck for a bakery for a while and finished high school. I got by. I was average and people liked me because I wasn't in a hurry to go places like my classmates who dreamed of going to Chicago or New York City.

The summer before I was to start classes at the local junior college, Larry came back to town. He looked stronger. His face was tan and he had this hungry look in his eyes that told me something had gone wrong out West. He'd been in fights, said a Mexican had tried to stab him with an apple knife and that he'd spent some time in jail. He got work at a garage in town and on the weekends he painted parking lots with one of his old high school buddies, a guy named Flip, who stuttered and smoked too much. Larry told me that it was just a job, that the work didn't matter to him, that he could rake coal in Hell if he had to.

I started college, stayed out late drinking with friends,

slept through classes and finally quit after my second year. Sometimes Larry would show up at my apartment and ask to sleep on the floor. When I woke in the morning he would be gone and I wouldn't see him for long stretches. He talked a lot about moving out West, maybe building a cabin or working in a pulp mill where he had a friend. Then he got himself arrested for setting fire to a 7-Eleven after the cashier refused to sell him beer after hours and made some joke how he was doing Larry a favor by not letting him drink. Mother used up what little savings she had for his bail and a lawyer. After all was said and done he drew a three-year sentence and went away to Lake State Penitentiary.

I went to work at Pea Lake Chicken Farms debeaking chickens. The pay was okay and when I came home I was too tired to do anything except fall into bed. I spent my days chasing birds down into chutes at the end of which was this machine that in one fell swoop cut and cauterized the beak, thus rendering the chicken harmless to its brother.

I worked the fryer barn where the skinny ones were kept, chasing and debeaking each new batch of chickens for most of the winter. On weekends I drove Mother up to see Larry. He was getting along okay. The hungry look was gone from his face and he spoke quietly about what he was going to do when his time was up. He said the worst thing was when he could smell the lake in the summer and how it made him think of all the stupid things he'd done to land himself in prison.

At the chicken farm foreman Tibbs could see the birds were getting to me and took it upon himself to move me over to the shit-cleanup team. It was a step up from debeaking. I worked under a man named T-Bone Thayer, whose job was to rid the farm of chicken shit, or "chicken gickem" as it was called. We bagged it for fertilizer, pumped it off into creeks, buried it, and still it seemed there could be no end.

T-Bone didn't talk much. The farm had broken him, made his back sway, his knees bow. His hands were thick and scarred from years of cold shovel handles and chicken wire. He listened to country and western on a dusty transistor he kept buried in his coveralls and walked the barn kicking chickens out of his path, running the drag rake behind him as the music blared from his pockets. Every now and then I'd catch him humming along to a familiar song.

I had my reasons for staying on at the farm. I suppose I didn't want to end up like my brother or father and I knew that I needed work—needed to come home bone tired and bitter.

That's how it was. The farm at 6:00 *A.M.,* home at four, television, beer, bed. A couple of years went by and the college kids started calling me a lifer behind my back. And I have to admit that part of me was thinking how easy it would be to just put in the years, snag a pension and be done with work. It was a life, a way through the world, not the best or most exciting, but I had money and a place to spend my days and for a while it seemed to be enough.

Then T-Bone hung himself.

A pudgy college kid called Joe found the body hanging from the tip of the front-end loader. He'd used a pile of chicken shit bags to climb up on and some baling wire for a noose. T-Bone's transistor radio lay at his feet still blaring out a static-riddled song.

A thin state trooper with mirror shades and shiny black boots pulled T-Bone down. Tibbs and I chased the chickens away from the body and tried not to look at T-Bone's blown eyes and pinched cheeks. One of the college kids puked when they rolled T-Bone onto a stretcher and his bowels let loose.

A week later I quit the farm. Lied about some bullshit big-money job and took my last paycheck. Larry was due to get out and I had it in mind to start up a little business of my own. I wanted something for Larry when he came out and I suppose maybe something for me.

So I bought a Ford Econoline van, filled it with drop cloths and roller pans and began to paint. It was easy work to get and I liked being alone in a room, putting the white on the walls.

Larry was released in June and we had a little party down at the lake for him. We cooked hot dogs and drank beer and planned our business. He said prison had given him time to think and that he wanted to do something with himself. I showed him the van, told him we could do okay if we kept working.

We struggled at first. The jobs were jobs other guys didn't want, like painting urinals at the bus station or scraping barns. But pretty soon it picked up until there was less and less time in between jobs and we took on laborers, college kids mostly, worked them until they quit. Then Trog came our way. Trog's real name was Richard and he hung on through every shit-eating job we tossed at him and became part of our crew. We listened to rock 'n' roll a little too loud, fought over who got to do the rolling and picked on each other to make the clock move. Trog took most of the abuse: a spackle knife raked across his knuckles, hammer whack to the knee, a screwdriver dug into the small of his back. Everybody got a little and with the threat of random violence, the radio on full crank and Trog hunting me down with a piece of conduit clenched in his fist, looking for payback on a crack I had given him with my five-in-one tool, the hours peeled by like summer days.

In an apartment on May Street working for this landlady who smelled like gin and wet dog, Trog ran the screw gun through a board and into my brother Larry's palm. I backed the screw out and wrapped a shirt around Larry's bloody paw. Trog ran off laughing and came back with a case of cheap beer to say he was sorry.

But just as things seemed to be going our way I could see my brother itching to put his nose into some trouble. Working like a dog and sucking paint fumes all day can make you want to do some crazy shit. We kept busy, though, and he came to work each day, put in his hours and went home.

But after a year something began to eat away at Larry. The radio bothered him. He came in drunk or high and dragged ass all day. Never a word about where he spent his nights. The joking on the job sites dried up.

I tried to keep him busy. Never the same thing twice. We went bowling after work and he got drunker than he probably should have. I pulled him out of a fight or two—one guy left bleeding, another with a few less teeth. I thought I could save him, snatch him away, but all we had was work and more work, not a whole fuck of a lot to be thankful or careful about. The worst that could happen was that he'd miss a day.

Right around August when it was too hot to work outside, we snagged a bid painting apartments for this landlord named Krebowski. Everybody called him Krebs. He had a funny accent and a lot of money. He went around all day checking on his properties, chewing Tums for his bad stomach and hassling people for late rent. His buildings were dressed-up turds, filthy beer-soaked dens in need of new carpeting and a brave exterminator, but there were always people willing to pay the rent.

It was a big job and Larry seemed happy to have the work. We signed to a deadline and moved our gear in, chasing one tenant out after the other as we moved from room to room. Trog taped, I cut and Larry followed behind rolling and humming to himself. We fell into a routine. Tool roll-out, clean, sand, tape, cut and roll.

But Krebs kept tabs, sneaking up on us while we worked, said he was keeping an eye out for his money, how it was being spent. And one day he caught us playing with the radio and arguing over the station.

"I pay good money," he said.

"Movin' and groovin'," I said, trying to ignore him.

Krebs looked at me and then Larry, who was slouched against a wall, cigarette hanging from his lips.

"I pay you top dollar for this?"

"It's break time," I said. "Leave the painting to us." I smiled.

Krebs nodded and began walking the apartment, inspecting the job, muttering to himself.

"I get complaints," he said. "The radio too loud, you guys banging around late at night. I want to know what's going on. My building. My business." He pointed into a bedroom that Larry had been working on the night before. There were stains on the wood floor, roller drift on the windowsill and places where Larry had just plain missed.

"Come here, you," he said, curling a fat finger at me.

Larry looked at me and held up his middle finger. His eyes were red and he had paint in his hair.

I walked into the room and stood in front of the wall with Krebs. Larry followed behind me.

"Here," Krebs said, pointing to long paint dribbles. "Here, here and here. What is this? I hope you fix. Good money for sloppy mistakes?"

Larry muttered something, went over to a can of paint, picked up his brush and stood there staring down Krebs, paint dripping all over the linoleum.

"Fuck the money," Larry said.

Krebs took one look at the paint on the floor and began to blow it in pinched English. "God. Stoopid. Muthafuckin' paint bastid." Krebs bit his knuckles.

Larry raised the brush and painted the word FUCK on the wall.

I tried to apologize, but it was too late.

He pushed me out of the way and got in Larry's face.

"Say Hail Mary," Krebs said to Larry. Larry lowered his mile-high stare at Krebs.

"Fuck Mary and fuck the job," Larry said. Trog tried to

step in between them, but Larry sent him to the ground with a forearm.

"Larry," I yelled as he pointed the paintbrush at Krebs, backing him down the hallway.

"No more paint. I fire you," Krebs said. "Fire. It's done —the contract void, finished."

Larry tackled Krebs and shoved the paintbrush into his mouth. Krebs flailed, his chubby arms becoming entangled in the canvas drop cloths.

When Larry let him up his cheap leather coat was covered with paint. "Out," Krebs spat. His words were white. I grabbed him and steered him down the hallway toward the door while Larry stood back by the roller pans swearing under his breath.

Krebs threatened to sue and in the end we lost a lot of other jobs. Larry no-showed for a solid week until I went looking for him and found him sitting in his apartment, a week's worth of beer and pizza boxes around his feet.

"You coming back?" I asked.

He switched channels on the television with the remote.

I asked him again.

"Don't know," he said. His skin was gray. His eyes looked blue and hollow from all of the television. A woman walked out of the bedroom with nothing on except an orange Cleveland Browns T-shirt. She had bad skin, over which she had smeared some makeup. Her hair looked slept in and she had black rings around her eyes. Larry couldn't remember her name.

"Judy," she said, sitting next to Larry on the couch.

"You want him to come back to work?" she asked.

I nodded.

"Stay out of this," Larry said to her.

She took out a cigarette and lit it.

"Sorry," she said. I could tell she meant it and I felt sorry for her.

"Krebs?" Larry asked.

"Lost it. The whole thing," I said.

"I figured," he said. I wanted him to apologize, but I knew he wouldn't.

"Trog is asking about you. Says he owes you a crack or two." Larry stared straight ahead, stuck two fingers in the air at Judy. She took one last drag and then placed the cigarette between his fingers.

"You know, that fucking job was just eating me alive. Felt like I was back in the hole again." Judy licked her lips and took the cigarette back from him. I could tell she liked the way he talked.

"Well, we still got work," I said. "If you want . . ."

"It don't ever stop," he said.

He wanted to say something else, but he stopped himself and put his fingers out for the cigarette again. The room was warm. The sun was coming through the bottom of the shades and it felt like I was someplace I wasn't supposed to be, seeing things I wasn't supposed to see. So I wrote down the address of our latest job site, a peeled-out printing mill that had been running Trog and me ragged. I set the address on the coffee table and let myself out. Judy waved at me and smiled.

Two days later Larry showed at the site. He looked better and Trog got him to smile when he threatened to kick his ass. We went to work without saying much, the sound of our tools filling up the silent mill.

I let Larry tape while Trog and I slogged through the last of the scraping. Every once in a while Trog scooted down the hall to check on Larry.

At lunchtime Judy came to the door with a bag full of beer and sandwiches she'd made herself. Larry let her in. She touched his face and hair before kissing him gently on the neck. Then she put spit on her fingers and rubbed the dots of paint away from his mouth.

"Brought you all something," she said. Her hair was done up in a bun and she had on some perfume that cut the smell of paint from the air. Trog rumbled out of the utility room, scraper in hand, and whistled. Larry went red and threw a screwdriver at him.

"Never seen a woman before?" Larry said.

I thanked her for the beer and pulled over a paint can for her to sit on.

"My name's Richard," Trog said. "But these assholes call me Trog." Judy laughed and reached out for Larry's hand. He brushed it away and she pinched his thigh until he took her hand.

"I just wanted to see what you guys do all day," Judy said.

"This is about it, same shitty songs on the radio, a little paint on the walls, sometimes Larry and Trog here go at it for excitement," I said.

"Miles and miles of smiles," Larry said. Trog nodded in agreement.

"So that's it, huh?" Judy said.

"I don't know why I came back to this shit," Larry said.

Judy frowned and both Trog and I looked at one another, trying to let the comment drop.

"Be done scraping today," I said, motioning for Trog to toss me another beer.

"Scraping's about the worst work I know," Trog said. He looked at Larry.

"Try waiting tables," Judy said.

"We don't need to hear about that," Larry said. "Let's just leave that alone."

"Where you wait tables at?" Trog asked.

"She waits tables at None of Your Fucking Business Lounge," Larry said.

He pounded his beer.

"Uh . . . where's that?" Trog asked, crossing his eyes.

"It's in Shut the Fuck Up Ville."

"What the hell's your problem?" I asked Larry.

"Not a thing—it's just that Judy didn't come down here for Q. and A. with Trog."

"I work at Four Bares," she said. "I cocktail."

Trog started to say something.

"I keep it all on," Judy said. "I mean I don't dance if that's what you want to know, Richard."

Everybody knew about Four Bares, the women who danced topless for tips, the fights, the watered-down beer and fat bouncers who carried blackjacks.

Larry said, "You didn't have to tell them."

"I'm not ashamed of it. It's no better or worse than painting all day."

"I used to date one of the dancers," Trog said. "Her name was Yulinda—I think her real name was Linda or Dawn—something like that. She was a real good dancer."

"Bullshit," I said to Trog, who had a history of lying about women he'd slept with.

"Fuck, Ben, just ask Judy about Yulinda. Go on, tell him," Trog urged.

"I think I remember her. Bottle blonde, right?"

Trog nodded.

"Used to dance over at the Landing Strip part-time, right?"

"That's her," Trog said proudly.

"So what's your point?" Larry asked.

"My point is that I had a real fine-looking woman for a while until her boyfriend came back to town and threatened to kill me."

"Frank Bottles," Judy said.

"Huh?"

"His name is Frank Bottles," she said.

"Big hillbilly motherfucker with arms like an ape?" Trog said.

"That's him," she said. Something in the way she spoke told me she had trouble at work. Maybe some trouble with Frank Bottles or some other piece-of-shit hanger-on. Things went quiet and a little later Larry sighed, pushed himself up off the floor and said it was time to get back to work. He walked her to the door. They had words, but I couldn't hear them.

After that Judy started showing up once or twice a week for lunch. Sometimes she'd be dressed in her work outfit, tight cutoff jeans, a cheap red T-shirt pulled over her shoulder and high heels.

Larry seemed oblivious. The job dragged and Larry kept quiet even when Judy came around. At quitting time he took off in his truck and there were times when I didn't expect him back in the morning.

The job moved along and finally we got to spraying the ceiling. Trog walked the line behind us brushing the dryfall into piles while Larry and I waltzed our way down the length of the building swinging the spray guns in wide arcs.

After two hours the fumes had us high. Trog was covered in drift, his hair frosted with dry paint. We took a long lunch and waited for the headaches to come.

"Well, I figure we just fucked a couple of years off our lives," Larry said.

"Maybe a month or two. Quit smoking and you'll break even," I said.

"Fuck, everybody's got to die somehow," Trog said.

"Judy coming by today?" I asked.

"No."

"Ice-cold beer would be the shit right now," Trog said.

"Go get some beer yourself," Larry said.

"I like it better when Judy brings it by. It just tastes better," Trog said, smacking his lips.

"Better watch yourself, Trog," I said.

"I don't wanna talk about her anymore," Larry said.

"What's the matter with you?" I asked. Larry rolled his shoulders, pulled off his mask. His whole face was white except for his mouth and nose.

"She lost her job," he said. "Lost her job and things aren't so good between us."

"What do you mean?"

"I mean just what I said. I don't know how to fix it. I

mean one more fuckup is all I get—so I guess I can't be Mister Fixit."

"She in trouble?"

"Club owner says he caught her stealing, not writing down drinks on her tickets."

"She can get another job," I said.

"That's not all," he said. "They want the money back. These aren't nice guys we're talking about. It's the sort of situation that calls for bad things. Know what I mean?"

"I don't," I said. "Leave it. We've got something here." I pointed at the new paint on the walls.

"And I give a shit?" he said.

"It'll pass over," I said, but Larry was already up fooling with the sprayer.

We finished off the rough stuff and worked on touch-up the rest of the afternoon. Larry kept quiet. He was chewing on things, weighing options. Even Trog left him alone.

We quit at sunset. Larry got into his truck and pulled out of the lot, gave us his usual wave out the window.

"What would you do if you were him?" Trog asked. He had a roll of electrical cord coiled around his arm. He was dirty and tired-looking.

"I think I'd probably keep driving," I said.

"Shit, he's your brother, maybe he needs your help."

I shook my head. I couldn't tell Trog how Larry would resent the help, that the only thing I could do was to sit back and let him twist in his own wind.

"Suit yourself," Trog said as he rolled up the last of the hoses and cords. "He's in trouble whether you like it or not."

"I don't know what to do."

"Doing nothing's worse," Trog said. "We need him."

I nodded and stomped on paint cans.

The next morning Larry didn't show up. I figured he was out there somewhere maybe driving like hell to dump us, the job, Judy and her troubles, or maybe, although I didn't want to think about it, he was somehow squaring Judy with the club owner. I knew he didn't have the money for the simple way out. Larry lived nickel to nickel and when there was some left over he spent it on foolish things, like carbide buck knives or new rims for his truck.

When we'd finished for the day Trog looked at me and said, "Well, what are you gonna do now?"

"Wait," I said.

Trog shook his head and left.

Later that night I got the call from Judy. She said I had to come right away, that there was some trouble. I clicked on a lamp, stared at the clock before crawling out of bed and pulling on some clothes.

Four Bares was closed. Larry's truck was double-parked at the end of the lot under a little fold of sumac trees. The whole place looked grown over and badly in need of some paint and good fortune. It looked like the sort of place you'd pay five dollars to watch a girl dance topless and have her look away when you told her you loved her.

I entered through a side door. Judy was sitting in a booth under a beer sign. She'd been crying. Another waitress or dancer, I couldn't tell which, was sitting next to her.

There was some music on low and two bouncers talking quietly by the stage.

"That's him," Judy said when I entered. This seemed to relax the bouncers. The place reeked of beer and sweat. Judy grabbed my arm and pointed to a door behind the deejay booth.

"Larry's in there with Hargrove and maybe some bouncer or something. They went in about an hour ago. I didn't know what to do," she said.

"That was a fool thing to do," I said. This set Judy to crying again. I could smell whiskey on her breath.

"He's been drinking and talking about how he was going to set things straight."

"Hargrove's the owner?" I asked.

She nodded. "It really wasn't his money, customers mostly—I didn't write things down on the tickets like we're supposed to. It's my fault."

I ignored her and went to the office door and knocked. I could hear voices and chairs scraping the floor.

After a minute the door opened. A small man in cowboy boots and tight jeans stood at the door rolling a shot glass in his hands.

"You the brother?" he asked.

I nodded.

"Roy Hargrove," the man said. He stuck out a soft hand for me to shake. His face was small, his skin tight against his skull, even the wrinkles were flat. He had on a string tie and a dark leather vest with a pack of cigarettes in the breast pocket.

He motioned me in. The office was small and square with low ceilings. Cigarette smoke hung in the air. The walls of the place were covered with Polaroid shots of the dancers and beer posters. There was a camera system set up with video monitors that blinked shot after shot of the bar.

Larry was sitting in a chair, his lip bleeding. There was a larger man, a bouncer, standing behind him flipping a broken pool cue into his palm. The bouncer was big in all the wrong places, neck like a stump, swollen hands, thick forearms and tiny little eyes set back against his nose like nail holes. There was a half-empty bottle of whiskey on the table and an ashtray full of crumpled cigarette butts.

Hargrove spoke first.

"Your brother here tried to come into my club." He paused. "My club, came into my club—after hours, trying to set some things straight."

"I'll take him home," I offered. I knew this wasn't going to do any good even though I figured Hargrove for a fair man on any night except this one.

"Ben," Larry said, "you shouldn't have come."

"It's a little too late now, isn't it?" Hargrove said.

"We can forget this," I said.

"Well, Ben, can I call you Ben? I thought so. I don't see any sense in Larry's head here. Seems to me, a smarter man, a man such as yourself, although brains tend to run in families—anyway, a smart man might say to himself that this is not the sort of thing to stick your nose into, especially when the issue doesn't really involve you. Would you agree with that, Ben?" He paused and fingered the shot glass. The bouncer sighed and shifted against the wall.

"Well, I'd say let's forget the whole thing and everybody just go home," I said.

"Fuck him," Larry said. The bouncer chuckled and

pulled the whiskey bottle off the table, took a pull and offered it to me.

"We can all agree I've got the money coming to me," Hargrove said. "I've got a business to run and I can't have some stupid-ass waitress who thinks she's too good to dance or show her titties take money from me, now can I?"

"How much does she owe?" I asked.

"No way to put a number on something like that, but if I were to ballpark, oh, I'd say several hundred. I've offered her the chance to work it off—dancing for the house. I'm not forcing anything on her. Just an option is all, the smart option. Makes everybody happy. I want you to know that I'm not an unfair man."

He pulled the pack of cigarettes from his breast pocket, shook one out and stuck it in his mouth.

"That's it?" I asked.

"Might take her a couple of weeks to get her moves down—tips are better that way. Lots of girls find themselves in similar circumstances, rent due, trouble, maybe they got a boyfriend who likes his cocaine, some just steal to steal, I suppose. At any rate—if I catch them at it or if I know they've got sticky fingers I give them options. You like options, Ben?"

I raised my hands up over my chest and the bouncer flinched himself forward a few steps.

"So the problem is that Larry here comes into my place of business and starts demanding things. Getting mental in my club like there's some kind of war going on I don't know about," Hargrove said. He pointed at himself and squinched his eyes for emphasis. I looked at Larry and knew that he was ready to pop. His eyes were locked dead ahead on the bouncer, who seemed to float between us.

Hargrove continued. "So Larry takes a swing at me. Can you believe that?"

"I'm sorry about that, Mr. Hargrove," I said.

"Don't be sorry. I slipped him, used to box in the navy, that's how I got this nose. So Scotty sees this happening and puts your brother down. Happens all the time in here, as you might imagine."

"Look, Mr. Hargrove, my brother's in no position to be causing trouble," I said.

"Well, it seems to have come to that, doesn't it?"

Suddenly Larry stood up from the chair. The bouncer rushed at him, clamped him back down into the chair and short-punched him in the mouth. His fist made a sucking sound against Larry's face.

"We don't want any more trouble. Maybe we can work something out," I said. Larry struggled against Scotty's grip. Hargrove sighed and looked at his nails.

"I just told you the options," Hargrove said.

Scotty looked up and smiled as he wiped his fist clean on my brother's hair.

"No fucking way she dances," Larry said. There was blood down the front of his chin. His lip was split to his nose.

Hargrove draped his arm over a file cabinet and pretended to yawn.

"Roy, you want I should toss this fucking bum out in the street?" Scotty asked as Larry struggled against the bouncer's grip.

Hargrove eyed me.

"Let him go a minute—see if he can behave himself. Maybe give him a drink of whiskey," Hargrove said.

Scotty shook his head, paused and then stood away from Larry. That was all Larry needed. He turned on Scotty and put him down hard with an elbow to the nose. Hargrove made a move at me. I ducked and shoved him into the wall. He threw the shot glass. It exploded against the cinder-block wall. Small flakes of glass rained down on us as Larry kicked Scotty to the floor and stood over him.

Hargrove shuffled through some papers on top of the file cabinet and came up holding a box knife. I backed off and watched as Larry ground the leg of a chair down into the bouncer's throat. The bouncer's whole body cracked and gurgled and then lay very still, there was a popping sound in his throat as my brother took the chair away. Hargrove went after Larry with the knife and managed to put it into my brother's side once or twice before I knocked him to the ground. The knife fell out of his hands and I kicked it clear.

Larry dropped to his knees, his hand clutching at his side and coming away red. I kicked Hargrove a couple of times and watched him curl up under the table holding his hands to his face. He looked small, like a sack of rags.

I helped Larry to his feet. He was bleeding bad and shaking. I knew we had to make it out the door quickly. The razor had opened up two long smiles of flesh on his side. Everything happened so fast and silent. I remember looking down at my brother's face and thinking to myself how sorry he looked just then, the way his eyes pinched up with every breath as if he wanted to say something, but couldn't.

Later, driving around town with Larry in the back seat, bleeding, Judy in front crying quietly, I knew that things had come to an end for my brother.

"We've got to get him to a hospital," I said. My mouth hurt and I could feel where I'd lost a tooth or two coming out of the office, meeting the other bouncers, who chopped and punched at us before the sight of their boss and Scotty lying on the floor drew them away.

Judy said, "He'll go away this time and never come back."

"Fuck the hospital," Larry spat. We drove past rows and rows of strip malls, empty parking lots and abandoned foundries. Judy rolled down the window. There were sirens off in the distance. The night air smelled like rust and smoke.

"I'm taking him," I said.

Judy looked up and nodded. There was no other way. We both knew what would happen as I turned the car around. When I looked back in the rearview mirror to check on Larry I couldn't see his face, only his hands, and they were still, calm even.

It's been two years since that night. Trog and I still paint like zombies. There is always work, more jobs than we can handle, and all of it's the same. On weekends we sometimes drive up to the prison and see Larry. He looks older and doesn't talk much. Judy stopped coming by after a couple of months. She dances now at the Four Bares and when I run into her sometimes at the store or some other bar she pretends not to remember. It's better that way. In the end Larry's cuts weren't all that bad. The doctors said he was a good healer—that his blood clotted up nicely. They arrested him in his bed and when he was well enough to be pushed out of the hospital they put him inside the county jail until the trial. I got off with two months and some community service. It was just enough to let me know that there are some things out there that can make you crazy and desperate—things worse than work, situations where you start to turn on yourself until there's nothing but trouble.

Now, when Trog and I are walking through the dryfall, the compressors grinding behind us, making things white, I know that this is what's good in my life, the clouds of paint, the blank walls and more work than I can handle. I don't think about Larry or my father or even Judy. People leave, but there is always the work and walls to make clean and white and that's what matters.

LAURA BOREALIS

It was close to the end of another brief Alaskan summer and winter was brewing up in the mountains, shortening the days and putting a general chill into the air at night. Leaves dropped, flowers browned and then fell into their bed. Mosquitoes died. The air smelled of smoke from woodstoves, and even the tourists who had spent the summer Polaroiding the shit out of the landscape were snagging their last spawned-out salmon or oohing and aahing one final time from climate-controlled buses at ready-to-hibernate grizzly bears. Meanwhile I was spending my afternoons at the

Boatel waiting for winter and counting what little money I had to my name.

Things were bad. I'd sold my moose-hunting rifle for four hundred dollars and a burnt-out drill press to this welder type who said he ran with the Hell's Angels, Fairbanks Chapter. I was answering ads for anything: counter help, security guard, responsible/go-getter, fishing guide and smoke jumper. Ads that read in capital letters: EARN$$—SKY'S THE LIMIT, and ones that promised fifty thousand in three months with, I quote, "maximum potential," even though I'd never earned more than twenty-five thousand in a year.

But I'd met this woman. It was noon and I already had a couple of drinks in me when she walked into the Boatel. She had long brown hair that put my heart on the floor and wide scared-looking eyes that darted around the Boatel's grungy interior like a cornered animal. She caught me staring more than a few times. It wasn't often that a beautiful woman walked into the Boatel in the middle of the afternoon. Available women in Fairbanks fell into three categories. The most visible were the beer-bellied, twice marrieds that prowled fishing derbys and saloons in search of husband #3, or husband #4. The second category, and perhaps the most dangerous of the three, consisted of the Recovereds and the zonked-out Born Again, God-is-great types who combed the bars handing out One-Day-at-a-Time and Easy-Does-It bumper stickers hoping to rope some poor slob into sobriety, steady employment, family and a mortgage with a little low-cut blouse action.

The third kind of "available" women were the exotic dancers—long-nailed, big-haired unobtainables who walked through town half-dressed, cutting out hearts and charging money.

After the first snow and until breakup, planeloads of strippers fly in to fleece horny, holed-up Alaskans with pole dances, pasties and tan legs at the Lonely Lady Good Time Saloon or Reflections, a scummy-looking Quonset hut of a bar that advertises itself as a place for couples. Strippers drank and fought like wildcats. They had nothing to lose; just three weeks to take off all their clothes and make fistfuls of money before flying back to wherever it was they came from in the first place—warm strip-malled cities like Tempe, Tucson or Tampa.

I didn't know how this woman fit into the grand scheme of Alaskan womanhood and frankly I didn't care. It was nice just watching her walk across the Boatel's buckled floor as she admired the moose heads and dusty bowling plaques that passed for decor. She looked sad and beautiful, and for a second I was Bogart sizing up Bacall.

Jim, I said, sticking out my hand. The name's Jim.

She said her name was Linda then gave me one of those lotion-rub handshakes before nodding at the bartender for a drink.

Schnapps, she said.

I pulled out the last of my money and pushed it across the bar.

Ahh, a gentleman, she said. Imagine finding one in here.

She knocked back her drink in two gulps and then proceeded to suck on the ice. I motioned for another one and the bartender gave me the credit signal. I nodded glumly and watched her drink, while all kinds of crazy thoughts jackhammered around my head. I closed my eyes and had one of those "first kiss to fuck to wedding to barefoot and pregnant" fantasies.

After some chitchat we played darts and then shot pool on the Boatel's ruined table, which more often than not doubled as a drink rail. I bought her more drinks with money I didn't have and before long we were kissing.

She tasted like peppermint schnapps and already I'd promised her a steak dinner at the Forty-niner Club. After that I didn't know what.

That's when Sammy Landewski blew in the door, bobbled his way up to the bar and started running his mouth about the old Williams lodge. Said he'd overheard some rich guy named Jaspers telling the cashier at the Grizzly Bear Grocery and Video Shack that he had big plans for the place.

Linda excused herself and wandered off toward the bathroom, lingered for a moment in front of the jukebox while some Loretta Lynn played to the near-empty bar.

Get the fuck out of here, Sammy said, staring at Linda's ass. She's with you? I don't believe it.

Sammy looked at me. I gave him a wink and nodded in Linda's direction.

Why not? I asked.

Ah, for Christ's sake, Jimmy, for starters she's beautiful, Sammy said. You want more reasons? I got millions.

She is beautiful, I said.

And she's with you. You hit a pull-tab? Win big at cards? Drug her?

I ignored him, thinking about Sammy's rich guy story.

You said this guy was looking for carpenters?

Sammy kept staring at the restroom door waiting for Linda to reappear. So I bought him a dollar draft and had him tell me the story again. He was a little foggy on whether the cashier had passed on any names. So I bought him another beer. You're going to have to do better, I said, dangling the beer in front of him, then taking a long swallow.

Marv Stacks? he said. Maybe she said Marv, hell if I know.

You mean Marv "The Hack" Stacks?

Sammy nodded and I shot out of my seat. Sammy seized on the opportunity to grab my beer glass and swill down the backwash.

Pretty sure it was Marv, Sammy said. Is she really with you?

I waved him off. Suddenly the curtain of alcohol parted. I saw dollar signs, and I looked around the bar for Linda and she was either gone or in the bathroom. I remember mumbling Marv's name over and over and the more I said it, the angrier I got that some cake job should fall into his unworthy hands.

I gave the bathroom theory ten minutes and when she didn't show and the jukebox ran out of quarters I sped over to the Williams place in my Ford, ladder racks rattling around every turn, nails dropping off the tailgate. I had the radio going full blast. The sun wasn't looking too good in the sky and every once in a while I thought I saw a snowflake trickle down through the pine trees.

When I got to the Williams mansion there were moving trucks and vans all over the place. Steroid cases in tight jumpsuits were hercing furniture and racing each other with dolly loads of cardboard boxes. An army of shirtless lawn boys with summer tans and headphones wrapped around their brains were pushing power mowers across the weedy expanse.

The place wasn't in such bad shape. It could have used a new coat of paint. There were some rotten clapboards and a pergola that looked more like a lean-to, but overall it was your standard-issue Alaskan twigged-out Tara: complete with split-rail fence, pole barn and log-rail porch.

I snapped on my tool belt, hoping to look official and ready for any project tossed my way, but the Boatel's cheap beer was doing a number on my head. I thought I saw a moose up on the ridge, but when I looked again it was just a piece of deadfall with ravens on top of it. Then I heard a voice call out over the din of mowers and weed whippers.

I turned and looked through the forest of furniture to see this stoop-shouldered guy waving at me. He had on a pair of baggy chinos and a golf hat pulled down low over his eyes that made him look like some gone-to-seed golf pro.

I worked my way through the furniture.

Can I help you? he said.

I asked him if he owned the place.

All of it, he said, raising his arms to show how much. The name's Jaspers.

He proceeded to give me one of those rich guy handshakes, like he didn't want to get his hands dirty but just the same was dying to show me what kind of grip he had. I told him my name was Jim and I'd heard he needed a carpenter.

He squinted at me from under his hat. His teeth were small and narrow and his skin looked as if it had been tanned and Martinized. He gave me a smile and hitched up his pants when he caught me staring at his Rolex. I figured him for oil money or investment banking. The interior was getting thick with these types lately. Rich dudes who spent the summers carting their friends and business partners all over Alaska in decked-out Land Rovers, shooting and hooking anything that moved. I stood there gawking at the watch thinking about the bad fuel pump on my truck and a bar tab at the Boatel.

Carpenter, eh?

I tapped my tool belt. In need of work and have references, I assured him.

Somebody beat you to it, he said.

He did a few imaginary golf swings before looking up at me. I squinted around for traces of Marv, his crummy van or his dog Milford. Nothing.

Big place, I said. You sure you don't have any work laying around?

This got him to thinking and rubbing his hands. Just then one of the movers interrupted us and asked him where he wanted the china hutch.

Dining room, Jaspers said, looking at the guy like he was retarded.

I got Marv Stacks working for me, he continued. Matter of fact he's out back working on the deck so I can have the hot tub installed. I got Texas-size plans for this place.

He rubbed his hands some more. I wanted to tell him

that Marv couldn't hang a prehung door to save his life, but I kept my mouth shut and stared him down.

I think he got sick of my staring because after a few uncomfortable minutes he said: What the hell. You up for a little competition?

Before I could consider my options, I was following him through the furniture, dodging movers, listening as he told me about his divorce and how he planned to have a little fun in Alaska.

Just before we got around back, I caught a whiff of Marv Stacks. Not really Marv, but Milford, who stank like dirty feet. Other than that he was a perfectly likable dog, came when called, loved to have his ears rubbed and fetch sticks. There were stories about Milford having once been a sled dog for Susan Butcher. But it was the stink that made him the most unpopular dog in Fairbanks, the sort of animal that set you walking in the opposite direction or caused women to snatch their children up into their arms. The problem was that Marv warmed his feet under Milford while he drank beer or watched television.

I was thinking about this when Milford trotted up to us, wagging his tail, just dying for any sign of affection.

Jaspers wrinkled his nose and retreated into a clump of elderberry bushes.

Marv, I said. Call Milford, will ya.

Marv looked up from his chop box, scowling at me before whistling for Milford.

After Milford had trotted behind the garage we gave each other the *High Noon* stare-down. Marv was a wiry little guy with nasty teeth and a mop of wild uncombed hair that he sometimes kept in a ponytail if the black flies weren't too bad. He wore a snowmobile suit even in the dead of summer and avoided soap, showers and baths. He was banned forever from fifty-nine of Fairbanks' sixty bars, for fighting and, I suppose, his lack of hygiene.

Marv, I said, tipping my hat at him.

I could see he was itching to pull his hammer and pound me back into whatever hole I'd crawled out of.

Fellas, Jaspers said, I see you two know each other.

We nodded.

Well, lemme tell you what I have in mind, he said.

Marv drew his hammer and waved it at me.

We had a deal, he said to Jaspers.

Jaspers smiled then tugged on his hat like he was used to squirming out of deals. He paused, taking a few more golf swings before looking at us and saying: There's plenty of work, boys. Daylight's burning and the hot tub's being delivered tomorrow. I've heard you can sit out in the water when it goes seventy below, he said.

Freeze your head off, I told him.

This was true. Last year around January they'd found several Japanese tourists with frozen arms or frostbitten ears sitting up near Chena Hot Springs. *The Daily News Miner* ran an article on how the Japanese considered it good luck to consummate a marriage under the northern lights.

The deck's ready for the damn tub, Marv said, pointing at his handiwork.

Jaspers looked at what Marv had wreaked upon the deck and stood there shaking his head. It was an abortion. None of the boards were straight, screws everywhere.

Really? Jaspers asked.

Just about, Marv said, admiring his work.

I rocked back on my heels, hoping Marv's glaring lack of skill would speak for itself. Jaspers went on explaining how he wanted a raised deck around the hot tub with railings and drink holders.

Marv took out a lumber pencil and tried taking notes on a piece of two-by-four.

Boys, Jaspers explained, I've got to be honest with you —I want to watch the aurora borealis with some half-naked women in my own backyard. It ain't much, but it's the sort of thing you do after your wife gives you the big D and hightails it out of town with another man.

Women? Marv asked.

Fleshpots, Jaspers said. This fella at the airport suggested I build a hot tub. He said the women up here get a little crazy in the winter, something about a vitamin deficiency from lack of sunlight. When word gets around I've got a hot tub, I'll be knee deep in vitamin-deficient women and I plan on drowning myself in polar pussy.

He pointed up at the sky as if he somehow had the power to make it snow.

I asked Jaspers if he wanted a fancy wraparound deck for exhausted hot tubbers to flop out on after they'd had too many bubbles.

He pointed his finger at me and said, You got it, bub. I want the deluxe model. Better make it sturdy and wide. I want drink holders, towel racks—hell, anything you can think of I want. I expect I'll be turning them away.

I don't think Jaspers had any immediate plan of action, like how he was going to lure women out to his place, and I didn't want to be the one to break the news to him about the forty-ninth state's lack of womanly resources. In a word, they were scarce.

Have at it, boys, Jaspers said, pointing to the deck. Just remember I'm the guy with the greenbacks—the boss, the big Kahuna.

I thanked him and went to work.

We didn't talk much. I cut and Marv nailed with something close to biblical fury. Nails flew everywhere. He had Milford trained to retrieve them.

I told him it was a nifty trick.

Eat wood, was all he said.

By dinnertime we had the wraparound built. It looked like shit. The cuts were straight, though, and Marv was already taking responsibility for the design. Not only was I getting used to his stink, but I found myself thinking that he wasn't such a bad guy. He was nuts about baseball and had one of those crazy memories for batting averages, rosters and ERAs.

After the movers had the furniture inside the house, Jaspers stumbled around back. He was drinking a beer and carrying the remainder of a six-pack under his arm. His hat was pushed back off his head and I could see his bald spot.

He set the beer down on the deck.

Drink up, boys, he said.

He handed us each fifty bucks and then an extra twenty to Marv for being the first on the job. There was a lot more where that came from, and I could see that Marv was thinking the same greedy thought. Milford yawned and rose out of the bushes followed by a cloud of gnats and no-see-ums.

Hell's bells, that dog needs a bath! Jaspers said.

Marv nodded and mumbled how he couldn't afford dog shampoo. Jaspers squinted at him and shook his head.

Here's ten dollars. Take the mutt to a car wash—whatever you gotta do, Jaspers said.

Marv took the money and smiled at me.

You boys want to work tomorrow? Jaspers asked, pointing at the pergola.

Both of us nodded.

I went straight home and forced myself to bed. The sun still wasn't setting until midnight, making it hard to sleep. I dreamt about winter and woke up shivering.

I had a feeling that Marv was going to try to out-early me on the job—bad-mouth my lateness to Jaspers with some greedy notion of grabbing himself a bigger slice of handyman pie. I couldn't blame him. Ever since he'd come to town he'd been scraping shit bottom to make a buck. He said he'd come from the Prudhoe Bay oil fields, but no one believed him because he was flat broke and not much good at anything. He had slept in his truck that first winter and nearly froze himself stupid until he managed to slap together a cabin north of the city on state land. The thing about Marv was that in some crazy fucked-up way he was hungry. I mean he had ambition, but didn't have a clue as to how to go about getting what he wanted out of life, and of course, Milford didn't help any.

The next morning, as expected, Marv was on the pergola, hammer in hand.

You're late, he said, sticking out his puny chest at me. I could smell that in his half-assed attempt to please Jaspers he'd dumped an entire bottle of cologne on Milford.

It was five in the morning and the sun was pretty high in the sky.

Looking good, I said.

It was the truth too. Marv had a talent for demolition. The pergola was about down and Marv had already started digging the footings. I told him I'd start pulling nails. He grunted something at me and continued working.

Jaspers came out of the house and pinched his eyes at us and said he couldn't understand how anybody in Alaska got any sleep with the sun shining all goddamn day. He sniffed the air and smiled at Marv. The cologne hung in the air like an oil slick.

I want one just like it, boys, he said, pointing at the spot where the pergola had stood.

After he left, Marv looked at me.

What the hell's a pergola?

You just took one down, I told him.

Do you know how to put one back together? he asked.

Carpenter ants were crawling all over his face and hands, feasting on his sweat. I don't know what was going through my mind, maybe I felt sorry for him, I don't know, but something compelled me to offer a handshake.

We'll work on it together? Marv said weakly.

Hell, we'll figure it out. It might even be fun, I said.

He thanked me and finally let go of my hand.

I told him to take a nap while I ran to the lumberyard. He nodded and began pulling off his work boots.

Come on, Marv, I said. Put your goddamn feet away or

else go soak them in the creek. It's too fucking early and I haven't eaten breakfast yet.

But I've got to air out my corns, he said, tossing a boot over his shoulder. Milford spotted Marv's bare feet and started doing backflips and barking.

I ran to my truck and grabbed a bag of kitty litter I kept in case of black ice.

Here, I said, handing the bag to Marv.

What's that for?

Milford was licking Marv's feet.

Dump a little in your boots, maybe it'll kill some of that stink.

That's not a half-bad idea, he said, brushing Milford away.

When I returned Jaspers was lounging on the front yard with a couple of his buddies. Both of them were old and tan like Jaspers. They had drinks in their hands, which they tipped in my direction. Jaspers introduced me as help and they laughed about it. There was a fat guy named Bryce, who had sharp brown eyes and hair the color of powdered donuts. He was dragging on a cigar and talking with his hands while Johnson, Jaspers' other buddy, hit golf balls into the bush.

Bryce yammered on about some hiker who'd been mauled by a bear north of Talkeetna. He lifted his pant leg to show Jaspers a scar he'd taken from a wild boar in Kenya, as if the two were somehow related.

I could tell they were fresh off the plane by the way they kept staring at the mountains and talking about animal maulings. It would only be a matter of time before they had their rifles out and were shooting at ravens and ground squirrels.

I left them and went around back and woke Marv. During my absence Marv's feet had managed to overpower the cologne. Milford seemed pleased, wagging his tail, grinning when Marv dug his heels into his belly. I told Marv to get his boots on and help me with the lumber. I watched and made sure he dumped a little kitty litter into his boots before lacing them.

Feels like sand, he said. I kind of like it.

As he spoke Milford eyed his boots and let out a throaty growl.

We unloaded the two-by-fours and lattice before getting to work on the pergola. I was determined not to let Marv's hacksmanship get the best of this project.

Marv botched the layout several times until we were pulling more nails than we were pounding but despite Marv's best efforts the pergola began to take shape. It wasn't as fancy as before, but it looked all right, and besides, Jaspers didn't seem to care about anything except his hot tub.

By the time the plumbers got the hot tub up and running, Bryce and Johnson had returned from poking around in the woods with their rifles, listing a squirrel and two small unidentified birds as their take.

Jaspers chased them down with a tumbler full of mint juleps and showed them the tub and how the water jetted around.

Big deal, Bryce said. I've had one since '84, they get moldy and cats piss in them.

You just wait, Mr. Negative, Jaspers said before plunging into the hot tub, clothes and all.

Watching Jaspers swish around in the bubbling water, I thought about telling Marv how a bath wouldn't hurt him, but he was under the new pergola, beer can in his lap, talking to Milford.

I watched as Bryce took off his shirt and pants and hopped in after his buddy, his gut hanging over his underpants like a bag of wet cement.

It's got water and it's hot, Bryce said, flubbing about in the foam, steam rising off his broad hairy back.

Where does a man find women? Jaspers asked me. Just point us in the right direction.

He was mainlining a mint julep and sputtering while Bryce splashed water at him.

Divorced, Johnson explained, pointing at Jaspers. Twenty years with the same woman. She nicked him for a million and then flew to Cancún with her plastic surgeon.

Jaspers tried to splash us but gave up and contented himself with flipping Johnson off.

Women? Jaspers said. I'm not getting any younger and I'm rich.

I told him if he wanted women, Los Angeles was a couple thousand miles south. Working for the man was one thing. I wasn't about to pimp for him and his rich buddies.

What about that place by the airport? Bryce asked.

Strip bar, I said.

Oh yeah, Jaspers asked, raising himself out of the water like a seal.

That's the Lonely Lady, I explained. Back when the town went boom with pipeline money they used to have strippers lined up on either side of the road in G-strings waving at the workers as they got off the planes. Even in the winter.

The Lonely Lady, Johnson repeated. I like it!

Hell's bells, Jaspers said. Strip bars are full of women—what are we waiting for?

What about the bear hunt? Bryce said.

Fuck the hunt, Jaspers said. You just can't wander off and go hunting without a license.

William, you're drunk, Johnson said calmly to Bryce. Guns and alcohol don't mix.

Bryce hauled himself out of the tub and stood dripping on the deck.

I want to go hunting, Bryce screeched. I didn't come all this way to sit in a hot tub.

Now, William, Johnson said. Who paid for your air fare?

Bryce cocked his head and stared at Johnson.

We can hunt tomorrow, Johnson said. If James wants to celebrate then we should celebrate. He patted the big man on the belly.

What are we celebrating? Bryce asked.

My divorce, Jaspers yelled.

Bryce nodded solemnly and looked out into the woods.

Boys, Jaspers said. Hop to it and get dressed. We're going to this Lonely Lady bar and see if we can't recruit a little poolside ornamentation.

Johnson rolled his eyes at me as if I had somehow become an ally in his struggle to referee between Bryce's bloodlust and Jaspers' desire to be knee deep in women.

Jaspers slipped out of the tub, pulled his wet wallet from his pocket and began placing soggy bills in my hand.

Party supplies, Jaspers said. We'll be back in a couple of hours.

Yeah, get lots of booze, Bryce said, slowly getting into the mood.

How much? I asked.

Enough to choke a horse, son, Bryce said, pointing at his stomach. I nodded and watched as they marched into the house to clean themselves up.

I counted the money while Marv circled me, excited by the prospects of a party. I told him not to get his hopes up, but it was too late. The idea of being invited to a party had gone to his head like cheap wine.

On the way to the store Marv sang along to every song on the radio and nearly got us arrested when he saluted a passing state trooper for no particular reason. We made it to the store and I pushed the cart while Marv shambled down the aisles pulling fifths of gin and scotch off the shelf. At the deli counter, while buying peel 'n' eat shrimp and king crab, I took a good look at my reflection in the glass and shook my head—I was one sorry pimping bastard.

When we got back to Jaspers' Marv slapped together a makeshift bar and uprooted a small pine tree to set on the deck.

For effect, he said, pointing at the tree and rubbing his hands.

I suggested that he clean himself up a bit. I even mentioned women several times in the same sentence, hoping that it might drive him bathward, but he was too busy feeding Milford king crab and cheese wedges to listen. After ten minutes Milford started arching his back and gagging until cheese and crab came back up and sat steaming on the grass. Marv stood over the dog yelling something about how Milford wouldn't know a good thing if it hopped on his ass and bit him.

A few beers later Marv mumbled something shifty and disappeared inside. When he returned I almost didn't recognize him. He'd showered, put on some of Jaspers' clothes, combed back his hair into one of those rock star hairdos, and even brushed his teeth. Milford sniffed around Marv's feet, not quite sure what to think.

You're going to get us in trouble, I told Marv.

Marv's head dropped as he looked himself over.

I wanted to look better, he said. You know—for the women. Who knows, maybe I'll turn over a new leaf. I didn't always used to be this way.

You'd better hope that Jaspers is too drunk to notice, I said.

You think? he asked.

You look good, I said. It was the truth. Outside of being a little skinny he didn't look half bad.

Marv smiled. For all I knew Jaspers and his bunch would get drunk and come home empty-handed. He wouldn't notice the missing clothes, and in the morning we'd be back working on some new project.

Marv was the first to hear the Bronco roaring up the gravel road. There were two cars behind them, doing fishtails across the grass before finally coming to a stop under a sorry-looking pine tree. Marv snapped into action, kicking a mixture of dirt and grass clippings over Milford's puke and tying the dog to a tree behind the garage.

Bryce was the first around the corner. He was drunk and had a woman tucked under each arm.

Boys, he roared, Meet Mindy Moose and umm . . .

—Katrina of the Klondike, the one on his left said.

Ahh, yes, how could I forget, Bryce said.

The women giggled and kicked their long dancer's legs into the air as if to say hello. Mindy wasn't much to look at—too much makeup and her hair seemed thin on top where a ratty-looking pair of velvet antlers hung above her ears. But Katrina was something else. She had long blonde hair that spilled off her shoulder and swam around her perfect ass. Her lips looked red and swollen, as if somebody had been kissing them all day. She wore a see-through body suit that showed off a deep seamless tan and thighs so tight you could bounce quarters off them. Marv took one look at the women and started stuttering. He raised his arms as if to say something, but Bryce redirected Marv's hand to Katrina's breast where it hung there like a spider.

Katrina looked down at Marv's hand on her breast and said, That'll be five dollars.

She stuck out her hand and rolled her fingers. When Marv didn't respond, she snapped her fingers impatiently at him until he reached into his pocket and placed a crumpled five spot gently in her palm.

Now that's a good boy, Katrina said, winking at Bryce.

Jaspers and Johnson had women with them and before they could introduce them I saw her. It was Linda from the bar and she'd been dancing. Her hair was covered with sparkles and she wore a fake bearskin rug. She turned to go, but Jaspers wrapped a skinny arm around her, dragging her to the deck.

They work for me, Jaspers slurred, pointing at Marv and me. I flashed a cheesy smile and she closed her eyes for a moment and nodded as if she was replaying our afternoon in the Boatel.

There were others, a bouncer named Grizz who had a thick rust-colored beard and a giant salmon tattooed on his forearm. He had brought along a nervous-looking guy who said he was a bartender. Grizz pointed at Marv's makeshift bar.

Start pouring, he said to the bartender.

Johnson brought out a boom box and flipped on a Tony Bennett tape while Jaspers cranked up the hot tub. Linda snuck over next to Mindy and the still speechless Marv.

Milford started howling.

Marv, Jaspers said. Can you do something about the dog?

Marv came out of his trance.

He's a party dog, just like his owner, Marv said, before whistling at Milford.

I helped the bartender pass around drinks. When I handed Linda a peppermint schnapps on the rocks, she looked the other way.

Jim, Jaspers said, grabbing my arm. Meet Laura Borealis.

He pointed at the sky and guzzled his whiskey.

It's a stage name, Linda whispered to me.

Get it? Jaspers asked. Laura Bor-e-a-lis.

Laura? I asked.

Does Linda Jones sound like a name for an exotic dancer? she replied. The club owner said I'd make more money with an Alaskan-sounding name.

Before I could say anything else she sat and crossed her legs. I sat down next to her, the bearskin rug tickling my ankles.

Don't get any ideas, she said. I was lonely, she said. Okay? Okay?

It's all right, I said. I know how you feel.

Then she told me that she'd just gotten off the plane from Seattle yesterday and had needed a drink to sort things out.

And now what? she said.

You're in Alaska, I said. Anything can happen.

You're telling me.

Jaspers was the first to jump into the hot tub. He stripped his clothes, grabbed a shrieking Mindy Moose, and fell into the bubbling water. Black eye makeup melted down Mindy's face. The satin antlers went soggy and fell around her neck, covering up her breasts.

Old farts are the best, Linda whispered to me.

I looked at Jaspers and his buddies, at their wrinkled smiles and gray hair, and knew she was right. Bryce was showing Katrina his wallet, and she was pulling crisp bills out and shoving them down the front of her body suit. Mindy Moose and Jaspers were feeding each other gin and tonics in the hot tub and Grizz was doing pull-ups on the new pergola. Every so often when the wind shifted a blast of Milford's hellish stink wafted over the deck, causing people to stick their noses into their drinks. He was barking up a storm, and Jaspers in his gin-addled state paused to remark that he heard wolves.

Even by Alaskan standards it qualified as a party.

Jaspers ran up to us wearing Mindy's antlers, shaking his shriveled arms at the sky yelling, I love Alaska.

Johnson had produced two rifles and challenged Grizz to a little sharpshooting contest.

I looked at Linda, the drinks had gone to my head, and my heart felt like it was filled with nerve gas as I watched her sipping her drink. I had to say something, make some sort of stab at getting back what we had that afternoon in the Boatel. So I mumbled something stupid about her eyes. Used to hearing compliments, she looked right through me as rifles cracked and blue gun smoke floated across the deck in thin clouds.

Let's start over, she said. From the beginning, right here. I don't know who left who the other day—it doesn't matter. I'm working.

Now? I asked.

Always, she said. You think I'd come here if he wasn't paying me?

I started to say something, but she put a finger to my lips and pointed at the party.

I looked at the carnage Jaspers and his money had wreaked upon the party. There was flesh everywhere—old skin touching new skin. Everything and everyone was for sale and Jaspers was buying. I didn't know what I expected, only that it somehow involved Linda.

So I went and made her another drink, cursing myself

for the corny crap about her eyes. There wasn't much left at the bar. The bartender was passed out and somebody had shoved a lemon in his mouth. Grizz was reloading his rifle over the man, dropping empty shells on his face.

You like the girls? Grizz asked. Me, I seen too much nooky, I'm like saturated with it. Now guns—I like guns.

Grizz grunted something else and threw a bottle in the general direction of Milford, who was still barking his head off behind the garage.

Goddamn dog, he said.

When I returned Linda had stripped to her bra and panties and was in the hot tub. The bearskin lay in a heap under Bryce, Jaspers, and Mindy Moose, who were passed out on the deck and snoring loudly. It was getting dark and this crazy light, the last of the midnight sun, was slipping over the rim of mountains. Everything was glowing. Even the trees looked like angels.

Come, Linda said, patting the water.

I handed her the drink before stripping to my underwear and sliding into the water alongside her. The water felt like a warm glove. I moved closer. The nape of her neck smelled like lemons.

I heard more barking, followed by the whine of a Skil saw in the distance.

Grizz stumbled across the deck.

That crazy Marv fucker's building a throne for Katrina, he said.

Sounds like he ran out of money, Linda said.

A throne man, Grizz said. A goddamn throne!

Linda cut Grizz a look and he snuck off to watch Marv.

I listened as she told me about the bad boyfriends, her

string of dead-end jobs, and how she liked the cash dancing brought in.

I could hear Marv, pounding nails into the throne.

Then I asked her if that day in the Boatel was a one-time deal.

We've got three weeks, she said with a smile. Three weeks and I get on a plane and go to the next town. She gave me a little squeeze and scissored her legs around mine.

I didn't know what to say, so I just let the water bubble between us.

She asked me what I did and I showed her my hands.

I'm a carpenter, I said, hoping she wouldn't roll her eyes or say something condescending.

You really work for him? she asked.

I need the money, I said, and she nodded like she knew what I was talking about. For one moment everything seemed perfect. I knew she wasn't acting or trying to tease money out of me and I was starting to think about my options again and how winter was coming and all those lonely, workless days spent staring at the snow through a bar window.

Just then Milford let out a strangled bark. There was a snapping sound followed by the frantic scratch of claws on wood. Milford had chewed free of the leash and was beelining it for the deck, jaws snapping, hell-bent on making up for lost time.

I yelled for Marv, but it was too late. Milford had slid into the hot tub and was bobbing around, trying to keep his head above water. Marv's smelly feet residue melted off Milford and into the water like shrimp boil. All I could do was grab Linda and pull her closer. Bryce and Mindy rolled out of their drunken stupor and started gagging. There was more yelling and gunfire. Somebody tried to pull us out, but we held on to each other.

Grizz arrived and started pointing the rifle into the hot tub.

Like fish in a barrel, he said.

Then he pointed the rifle at me.

Just say the word and I'll put that stinky fucker out of his misery. It's your move, Grizz said.

I looked up into the sky, daring winter to come down from the mountains and snow on us. I knew then that happiness wasn't a job or even a place; it was sitting in a hot tub with a woman who called herself Laura Borealis, money in my pocket, three weeks to make her stay and a gun pointed straight at my heart.

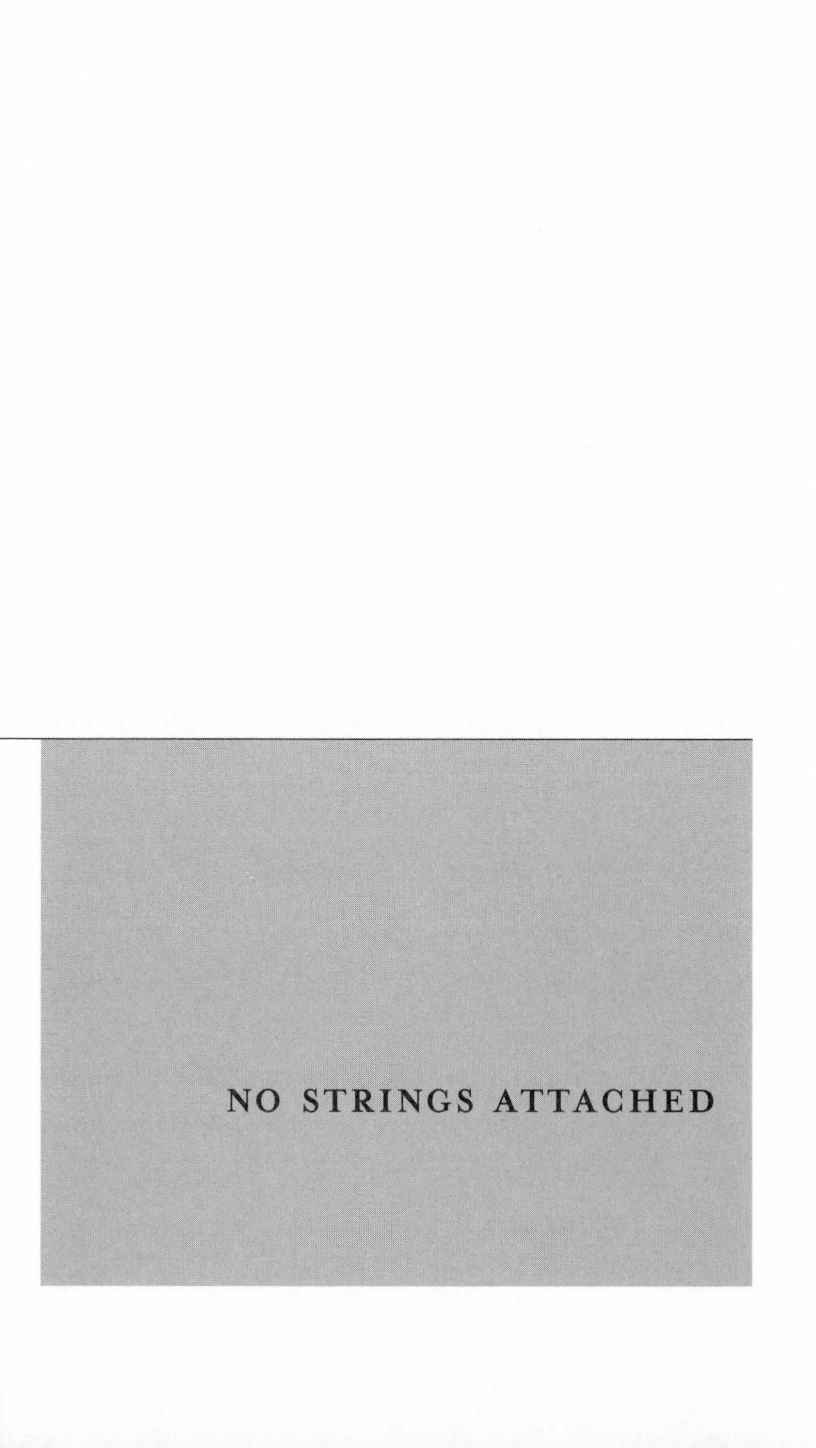

NO STRINGS ATTACHED

Friday after work I went to Krogers to put a few things in the fridge for the weekend. The parking lot was covered with broken bottles, smashed fruit, discarded receipts and candy wrappers. Shopping carts were scattered around the double-parked minivans and Hondas. The retarded kids the store hires were chasing down the carts in packs, herding them like cattle into chutes and then long lines. They were sweating and shouting to each other in some unintelligible language. It looked like fun until I saw a pale middle-management type standing on the cement pad, taking notes and shaking his head at the spectacle. I walked past him, through the automatic doors, and grabbed one of those dirty plastic baskets that announce you as a bachelor or someone in a hurry.

I was both.

But then I saw her. She was standing in front of the meat counter waiting to buy steaks in a crushed-velvet dress that was some shade of red I'd never seen before. I am a crushed-velvet man. I am also partial to silk underthings and long nails. Who isn't? So I stared at her. She had blonde hair with dark roots and the skin around her mouth was a bit wrinkled.

She rang the service bell and asked me what I was waiting for.

"Rib eyes," I said. She nodded, did something with her tongue that I liked.

"They're the best," she said. "You going to grill them?"

What could I say?

"Yes," I said, as she rang the bell again and smiled at me. She had long teeth. I looked in her cart. A plastic bag full of tomatoes, cotton balls, three large Spanish onions and some toothpaste. I had a six-pack of beer, a bag of oranges, gum and deodorant soap.

"It's the marbling," she said.

"Excuse me?"

"The fat makes the meat taste better."

The butcher came out from the back wiping his bloody hands on his apron. "Who's first?" he asked.

We both pointed. He looked at the woman and nodded. His face was broad, his ears smashed against his skull. He had gray teeth and small eyes that darted up and down her body as she indicated two steaks up against the glass. He sighed and bent into the case, pushing aside a strip of fake green grass. He grabbed the meat. His thick fingers dimpled the flesh and blood seeped under his fingernails.

After he handed her the package he turned to me, the smile gone from his face. "What do you like?" he asked.

I heard her cart rattle down the aisle behind me and I wanted to look back. I got one rib eye and asked him to trim some of the fat off. He rolled his eyes, grabbed a white-handled knife from a rack behind him and quickly pared a half moon of fat from the meat, dropping it into a bucket under the table labeled SCRAPS. Then he wrapped and priced the steak and handed it to me.

"Me," he said. "I eat what I want. Enjoy life, right?"

I thanked him for the meat and free advice and turned to go. Halfway down the frozen-food aisle I caught up to her.

"Just one?" she asked, staring at my basket again. I knew what she meant. It had been a long time since I'd been with a woman.

Before that it was Lydia. I wasn't exactly over her, but I knew enough to stay away. Lydia was hard and thin. She had dark eyes that could stare holes in you. She liked to party, drink ice-cold white wine, chop lines on Fiesta Ware and snort them with metal straws. In the morning, when the headaches came we ate crosstops for breakfast and fought. She blamed me for her lack of direction in life, that before she met me she was going places. Needless to say, I missed a lot of work when I was with her. I couldn't stop myself. Being with Lydia was easier than love—it was fun in a burn-up-all-your-tomorrows sort of way. Just when

I'd resolved to leave her there would be nights when the sheets were cool and we'd fought through most of Leno when she'd put her hand on my stomach, move it up and down and call me her "poor baby" and I would lift her nightgown and pull her on top of me.

She left me for the guy who fixed her Volvo. I came home one day after work and she was gone. His name was Bobby. He had tattoos and a thick fighter's face that on a good day made him look rugged instead of mean.

I decided to get clean, not double-A daddy clean, but I no longer called in sick and didn't need television or pills to make me sleep. I started running after work and promised to eat better, cut the fat from my diet and take vitamins. I wanted to live to be a hundred.

"You there?" she said, waving her hand in front of my face.

I nodded. The store suddenly seemed empty. The only other person I could see was this fat guy stocking frozen peas into the freezer, humming to himself.

"Only one," I answered.

"Want some company?" she asked, running her tongue across her chapped lips.

"What do you mean?" I asked. It was late and the Muzak version of Barry Manilow's "Mandy" was straining out of the store's PA system.

She looked at me and winked. "I mean," she said, "we go to my place have ourselves a little barbecue. We're both adults."

"Sure," I said, not knowing what I was supposed to do next.

"You don't recognize me, do you?"

I looked around behind me and then back at her. My chest tightened as I shook my head.

"Oh, come on," she said, patting me on the arm. Her hands were warm and I could feel the coolness of the rings on her fingers. "You're Gary."

"I've never seen you before," I said.

She smiled and waited until a tired-looking mother dragged her cart past us. There was a dark-eyed boy hanging out the front, holding a box of cereal aloft and shrieking.

"I'm a friend of Lydia's," she said.

I looked at her. I had never met any of Lydia's friends and on the rare occasions she mentioned them I had ignored her.

"We've met before?" I asked.

She nodded. "At the picnic. My name's Camilla. You played Frisbee a lot and Lydia said you were fighting."

"Well," I said. "Lydia and I are no longer . . ."

"I know. To tell you the truth, Lydia and I don't speak much anymore."

I smiled, relieved, waiting for some cue from her.

"You like your steak rare?" she asked.

"Moo," I said.

"I'm going to grab some wine first," she said.

I followed her to the wine section and drifted over to the dairy case, trying to remember if I needed cream cheese or half-and-half. Instead I selected a wedge of Maytag blue and some soda crackers. I was thinking, wine and crushed velvet and her mouth full of those straight white teeth.

My trance was broken by a clinking behind me. I turned to see her tapping her rings against a bottle of Cabernet. Lydia only drank white, said it tasted like melting snow and that red wine made her feel heavy and sad.

"You ready?" she asked.

I followed in my truck. I was pretty sure I'd never seen her before and that I'd never been to a picnic in my adult life. But there were a few fuzzy times when I got a jump on the vodka and tonics early and Lydia would just drive me around town, looking for somebody to buy pills or an eight ball from. I didn't care about anything. It was her adventure and I was Rolf Wutherich to her James Dean. People saw us coming.

Camilla's house was a large two-story clapboard with a wraparound porch, lilac trees and a crooked garage that looked as if it might collapse at any moment. I pulled in behind her and got out. The streetlamps were just coming on. I could hear children playing in the distance and there was the smell of charcoal and lighter fluid wafting across the whole neighborhood. She looked at me, her arms full of grocery bags, and bit her lip. Her eyes were soft around the edges, not hard and black like Lydia's.

An hour and a half later we were on her couch, eating store-bought berry pie off of thick plates and finishing the last of the wine. She leaned over and kissed me. I'd been waiting for this all through dinner, stumbling around the kitchen as she cooked and marinated the steaks, shaking when she touched my arm or gave me one of her looks that said good things were to come.

She had her hands on my stomach and was untucking my shirt when I heard a thumping sound coming from somewhere upstairs. She pulled away.

"What was that?" I asked.

She recovered and kissed me again. All sorts of paranoid thoughts raced through my mind: biker boyfriend, jealous husband, crazed serial killer partner, etc. For a moment I thought I would pay for my indiscretion with my life or the very least some bodily harm. But that only made it seem more enticing.

She seemed to be in a hurry and before I knew it she'd pulled her dress down around her hips and my pants were undone. There were no more thumps and as my hands moved to her breasts I wrote the thumping off as a door blowing shut.

"Mmm," she said, pushing herself away from me. "Condom." She went upstairs and I heard more creaking and thumping. Outside, the streetlamps were being smothered with clouds of insects and I could hear the splat of a nighttime sprinkler coming from somewhere next door. I thought about leaving several times and going back to my empty apartment. What stopped me was that I wanted a good time without Lydia and the fighting, the drugs.

When Camilla came back I was down on the carpet staring at the pattern of light that crisscrossed the ceiling. She stood over me and the room went black. "You ready?" she asked, dropping a condom onto my bare chest and lowering herself onto me until I could feel the heat coming off her. I never answered.

There was the normal awkward silence when we finished. She got up to go to the bathroom and then I got up to go to the bathroom. It was dark and we sat on the couch. She turned on the television and let the blue light of commercials and rerun sitcoms soak our skin. She fell asleep curled up on the couch under a lime green afghan. Sometime after midnight I dressed and slipped out the door and into the dark.

The next day I went by Lydia's apartment and rang the buzzer a bunch of times. I didn't want to see her, but after lying awake all night thinking about Camilla I had to know more about her, even if it meant dealing with Lydia again. And I suppose I wanted to gloat.

She answered the door in a bathrobe. Her face was pale, her eyes swollen.

"Jesus," she snorted. "Who went and made you the early bird?"

I hadn't showered and I could still smell Camilla on me. It was Saturday and I didn't have to be at the plant until Monday and nothing Lydia could say or do was going to kill my buzz.

"Mr. Volvo here?" I asked, trying to look past her.

She shook her head and stood away from the door to let me in.

"He's gone," she said. I entered and stood in the kitchen with her. There were empty beer cans near the sink and a bag of potatoes with the eyes growing out toward the window, pale and full of hope.

"Gone, gone?"

"I wish," she said. "The sonofabitch is taking me for granted. Can you believe that?"

I didn't answer. "What do you want?" she asked.

"You know Camilla?"

She went and sat down at the table and rubbed her nose before lighting a cigarette. "Yeah," she said. "What about her?"

"I ran into her yesterday, she said you were friends."

She rolled her eyes at me. "Don't believe everything you hear." She paused to drag on the cigarette. "Is that what this is about?"

I nodded. "Well, I ran into her . . ."

"Did you sleep with her?"

I looked down at my shoes and I don't know why, but my hands started shaking. I watched her smoking and knew that if she were to reach across the table and touch me, I would want to sleep with her. But then she stubbed out the cigarette and glared at me.

"You dumb bastard," she said. "Did she tell you?"

"Tell me what?"

"About her husband. Jesus, Gary."

Lydia stood there smirking at me. I could see she was pleased with herself.

"Husband?"

Then I remembered the thump when Camilla had first reached for my jeans.

"I'll let her tell you. We aren't really friends, you know.

I owe her money or something like that. Hell, I owe every-body. Besides, she's a friend of Trina's."

"She's got a husband?"

"Sort of," she said. "Ask her—you think I'm making this up?"

I shook my head no.

"Well then, wipe that stupid lost puppy look off your face. I know why you came by—you men are all alike. If you only knew how obvious you all are. You want me to feel sorry for you."

"No," I said. "It's not like that."

She laughed and lit another cigarette, rolling her eyes at me. What I wanted to tell her was how bad she looked, how I was done with the late nights and just maybe Camilla was going to turn out to be something good for once.

"Are you okay?" I asked.

She tilted her head at me. "Look, Gary," she said, blow-ing smoke at the ceiling. "It's early and, yes, I'm okay. It's just I don't expect ex-boyfriends for breakfast."

"I'm sorry," I said.

"Of course you are," she said.

I got up to go and she followed me to the door, wincing when the sunlight hit her face.

"Camilla's an okay person," she said quietly. "Just ask about her husband is all, before you start getting all lovey-dovey."

"I don't know why I came here."

"Of course you don't," she said. "But it's okay. Just call next time."

She reached out to put her hand in mine.

"You miss me?" she asked in her little girl's voice.

I knew I shouldn't answer that one. Instead I untangled her fingers and walked out the door without saying good-bye.

I went back to my apartment and listened to Tom Waits all day until my head hurt. Then I put on some Sinatra, took a shower and went over to Camilla's place.

"Hey, stranger," she said. She was weeding a flower bed on her hands and knees. Her arms were covered with dirt and her hair was stuck to her head with sweat. I wanted to kiss her—roll around in the grass with her. I could hear the Sinatra in my head and I felt like a lover.

Instead I stared at her until she stood, a clump of weeds clenched in her right hand like a severed head.

"I talked to Lydia," I said.

She pushed her hair out of her face and she was pretty again, in a tired, end-of-the-day way. She stopped smiling and let the clump of weeds drop.

"And she told you?"

I nodded. "Is he watching us now?"

"It's not like that." She paused and took a deep breath. "You want to meet him?"

My chest tightened and I knew there were a lot of wrong things to say, so I said nothing and stood there trying to remember how her skin felt on mine or the way the carpet smelled when she pushed me back to the floor.

"She didn't have to tell you. I mean we had fun, didn't we?"

"But," I said.

"Always a but, isn't there?"

I nodded.

"Come," she said. "It's better I show you."

I followed her into the house. The sheet on which we'd made love was still on the floor, tangled and twisted. The house smelled of sunlight and bath oil, not at all like Lydia's sour apartment.

She stopped at the foot of the stairs. "Promise you won't run?"

"I can't promise anything," I said. She made a sad face and continued climbing. She came to a door and pushed it open. I could hear the whir of machines like insects as a blast of cool antiseptic air rolled over me. There were thick curtains across the windows and it took my eyes a minute to adjust to the dark.

In the center of the room was a large hospital bed surrounded by machines with red numbers and tiny dials. Cords and tubes ran from the machines to a lump on the bed. She went over and put a hand on the lump. Something moved under the blanket and I stepped back to the doorway trying to find a window with some natural light streaming through.

"Gary," Camilla said. "I'd like you to meet Richard."

I moved closer until I could make out the frame of a man under the sheets. His body was curled in on itself like a sardine tin lid and his arms seemed to shake slightly as if he was cold. I looked down into his face and could tell that it had been handsome, but now it was pale and splotched with small pink irritations. My eyes kept tracing the impossible curve of his torso, lingering on the unnatural bend of a leg or the soft white gnarl of an exposed forearm.

She clicked on a light next to the bed and pushed a button that made the mattress tilt.

"There was an accident," she said. "He can't talk or do lots of other things."

She sighed and fiddled with a dial on one of the machines.

"Can he hear me?" I asked.

"Maybe," she said. "But I don't know if he understands. You can touch him. He responds to that."

I thought, who doesn't respond to a pretty woman touching him?

"You want to know, don't you?" she said. "First they stare, then they want to know."

"Okay," I said.

"It was snowing and he was late coming home and drunk. He went to pass this truck and his car hit a patch of black ice and slid into a tree. They had to cut him out of the car. He was in a coma for a long time. They gave me odds and percentages, but I was young and they didn't mean anything to me. We'd only been married a year. He was this big healthy guy—worked in the foundry and rode motorcycles—and I thought that he was invincible. The way he walked, I mean he filled up a room. He was so strong. I thought people like that lived forever. But I was wrong. There was an infection, a complication from all of the surgery, and his head filled with fluid."

When I asked her why he wasn't in a home her shoulders slumped and her face seemed to relax.

"Have you ever been in one of those places?"

I shook my head.

"It was horrible. So I arranged to bring him home and it's been okay."

She paused. She wanted me to say something—stop her from talking, but I didn't.

"You have no idea what it's like," she said. "Nobody does. I bathe him and feed him and poke needles into his arm. It's been five years and there are times when I'm cleaning out the bags of shit and fluid that I don't feel like myself anymore. I try, but it's so hard, even the little things like going to the store. I want to feel happy and not have this burden. Then I get angry and I want to blame somebody, but there's nobody to blame. That's what I can't live with. So when I saw you in the grocery store, I thought to myself, 'Why not? Why shouldn't I have a little fun and not feel guilty about it?' "

I didn't know what to say. All I could do was stare and try to imagine this curled-up piece of human sitting up from the bed and walking. How he would want to kick my ass for fucking his wife. I could hear his breath moving in and out of his lungs. I moved closer to look at his face again and the eyes I thought were full of something just minutes ago now seemed blank. It was like staring at my own reflection in a dark window. I jumped when she touched me and tried to push her hand away.

"Come to me," she said.

For a minute that small little hump of a brain stem buried under all the gray stuff left over from when we were lizards and toads began to think—screw right here, right now. Why not? What's he going to do about it? Sleeping with Camilla under the glow and hiss of the machines and the dead gaze of what used to be her husband would be kinky, dangerous even. But then I looked at him again, walked out of the room, down the stairs, got into my truck and left. When I got home I put on my shoes and went running until my legs were numb and my chest burned and it was all I could do to peel off my clothes and fall into bed.

I couldn't stop thinking about that moment beside the bed when she'd leaned into me and put her hand on mine. What she'd wanted was a hug, some reassurance, and I had fled. No matter how many times I replayed the scene in my head I came away a bastard. It was all I could think about at work. And on Friday, just when I thought I could slip back into my dull routine, I arrived home to find my window broken and a note tacked to the door. It read: "We've got to talk. Call me!!! Lydia."

I threw it away, drank half a beer, poured the rest down the drain and taped a bath mat over the broken window so the mosquitoes wouldn't crawl in and went to bed. I woke to the sound of an engine revving outside my bedroom window. I parted the curtain. The parking lot was dark but I recognized Lydia's Volvo next to the telephone pole. I could see the soft red glow of her cigarette moving through the windshield and I knew she wanted me to go out there and invite her in. But I made myself stay in bed. She kept it up for another hour until the sun started to break over the horizon and I could hear birds. It was Sunday. I had work the next day and Lydia was stalking me.

An hour later I got up to eat breakfast and was interrupted by a knock on my door. When I swung open the door Lydia stepped into my apartment. Her hair was wet as if she'd just showered and she looked different, softer somehow and a little scared. I pointed at the bath mat covering my window and she winced.

"Sorry," she said. Her hands shook as she sat down. "I need help."

"So you toss a rock through my window and sit out in the parking lot all night?" I asked.

"Bobby and I had a fight last night and I sort of lost my head."

"And?" I said.

"I need money. I owe him money and I want him out."

"Get out," I said, pointing at the door. I expected her to scream or throw something at me. Instead she stood and nodded.

"Please, Gary," she said. "I don't know what I'm doing anymore. When you came over the other day, that's when I knew—we were good. I felt like we were going places, you know."

Before I could reply she pressed herself against my chest. I could smell wine on her breath and I tried to raise my arms and hug her but I couldn't. The wind blew and the bath mat made a flapping sound as she wrapped her arms around me, kissing my neck and running her tongue across my throat. She was crying and I could feel the tears dampening my shirt. I began to think how easy it would be to touch her back—lead her into the bedroom, take her clothes off and not say a word. Afterward we could get drunk and drive around like old times.

When I didn't move Lydia shook me. "Come on," she said.

"No," I said.

Then I heard a car pull into the lot followed by a door slamming. Lydia must have heard it too because she let her hands drop and stood there staring at me.

I went to the door in time to see Bobby coming up the stoop. He saw me and stopped.

"Lydia in there?" he asked. His face looked thick and mean.

I nodded.

"Out of the way," he said.

I stood there. I could hear Lydia behind me.

"Bobby," she said. "This isn't about you."

He looked at me.

"You've got until three," he said.

"And?"

"One," he said. Then he punched me in the face. I staggered out the door.

He stood over me. "You want two?"

Lydia screamed and rushed at him, her arms flailing in front of her. My cheeks felt hot and the right side of my jaw throbbed. I fished my tongue around inside of my mouth to survey the damage and came up with a small piece of tooth that tasted like gunpowder. I put the piece of tooth in my shirt pocket and listened to Lydia yelling at him. He tried to hug her but she scooted past him and ran for her car.

Bobby looked at me, his face slackened. "She ain't worth it, is she?"

Before I could answer him he was running across the parking lot toward her car. The crazy bastard loved her and I wasn't about to stop him, so I crawled back inside my apartment and shut the door and went back to bed. When I woke my whole head hurt and I knew that I wanted to see Camilla.

By the time I arrived at Camilla's my face had stopped hurting but I could taste blood in the back of my throat and the chipped tooth ached. I should have stayed home with a six-pack on ice. I should have done a lot of things, like drive to Lydia's and smack Bobby with a piece of two-by-four. Instead, I parked in front of Camilla's house and watched some neighbor kids jump through a sprinkler.

I went to the door and knocked. She answered and let me in. There were pill bottles and rubber gloves scattered on the kitchen table, the garbage was full and there were flies on the ceiling.

"And this means?" she asked.

I shrugged.

"You got questions—ask them now," she said. I could tell she was angry and didn't want to look me in the eyes. And I remember feeling pretty crazy, like a few bad turns and I could be chasing down shopping carts at Krogers, doped to the gills on antidepressants, happy to have a job.

"You do that often? That's all I want to know."

"What?" she said.

"Pick up men at the meat counter and take them home and screw their brains out with your husband upstairs?"

She smacked me and then grabbed my arm like she wanted to do something else to make me understand.

"Twice," she said. "And they never came back. They disappeared like it never happened. I didn't want them to."

"What?"

"Come back, you know. But you . . ." She didn't finish

her sentence, and I stood there rubbing the side of my jaw wondering why I attract women who are as likely to hit me as kiss me.

"But I'm here," I said. "And so is he."

I pointed upstairs.

"It's okay," she said. "There's room for two."

"I didn't mean it that way."

"And Lydia?" she asked.

"What about her?"

"I just want you to know what you're getting into here. I mean, the other day after you left I kept hoping you'd come back and when you didn't it was still okay. I have this . . ." She pointed at the house around her and I knew what she meant. "And it's my life for better or worse and I can live with that."

I nodded as if we'd just agreed on something and we sat down and had tea in the kitchen. She brought out some day-old coffee cake that washed away the taste of blood from my mouth. In some small way she was taking care of me and I liked it—I needed it.

"I told him about you," she said.

"Everything?"

She nodded. "I make it like a story and I tell about my life."

"I can't imagine," I said. She looked at me like she might smack me again.

"I'm not asking—" Then she sighed and looked out the window and I tried to look indifferent, although I wanted nothing more than for her to touch me. I didn't care about the husband. It was just one of those weird things in life you get used to. I mean, what's normal?

I reached for her arm.

"What do you want?" she asked. I shrugged and pushed my tongue into the cracked molar. It felt good. She turned her chair, leaned into my lap and put her hands on my thighs. She kissed me and my tooth stopped hurting.

"I like this," she whispered. I put my hands on her blouse and looked at her for some sort of sign. She nodded and led me upstairs to her bedroom. There were books stacked to the ceiling, blocking the windows, and photos on the dresser covered with a thick layer of dust.

"Are you okay with this?" she asked, sitting on the bed.

"What?" I said, as I watched her arch her back and peel her jeans off. Her eyes were closed as she pulled me down next to her.

"Me, him? I mean, this isn't exactly what you had in mind, was it?"

"It doesn't matter," I said.

"Of course it does. Everything matters. I told him about you." Then she kissed me and put my hand between her legs.

After we'd finished and she was asleep I pulled my clothes on and went out into the hall and looked into his room. The whole house was quiet and I stood there a minute, waiting for him to move. When he didn't I entered. He wasn't sleeping and his mouth looked different than I remembered, as if he had been smiling. There were tubes and wires hanging from the machines that were attached to him and as I watched him breathing I looked into his eyes, half hoping he'd blink or look away. He didn't. He held my gaze. I touched him. His skin was soft and warm. It wasn't like I thought it would be. Nothing was anymore. I was here in his room. I'd just been with his wife and it was okay. Everything was okay. I knew what I wanted and what I didn't want. I told him this and he didn't blink, not even when I reached into my pocket, pulled out the chipped tooth and set it in his palm. It was a piece of me and it meant something, only neither of us knew what and it didn't matter. I knelt there looking out the window until I felt his fingers move against mine. When I glanced back down I noticed that his hand had closed over the tooth and I couldn't see it anymore.

I lifted my hand away and returned to the other room to be with his wife.

RANDOM BEATINGS AND YOU

The tests at the VA hospital did not go well. The nurse was a butcher, couldn't get the needle right. A vein in your arm collapsed, which leads you to question whether or not this is any way to make a living. You are a carpenter who can't stand work. It beats you, makes your hands hurt, your ears, back, neck, even your fingernails, which take sliver after slam after stub. There are, however, five crisp twenty-dollar bills in your pocket. You are in a bar. You have a drink and the drugs they tried on you this time have given you a raging hard-on as well as a headache. That is why you are at the bar, drinking vodka and tonics (more vodka, less tonic). It is not your favorite bar. It is peopled with defectives and men in suits hiding out from their jobs.

You know two people in the bar and like neither of them. The bartender is a bar-tanned pretty boy—coke-red nose and twitchy eyes. He talks too much and pours light. To your left is a man in a suit who smells of aftershave and cigarettes. And to your right is Angel—one of two people you know but don't like. Angel is big and black. He has tattoos, no front teeth and you have been told his cock is pierced. He is the Picasso of drink chiselers, his talent is sniffing out coin.

When he spots money he says, "Yeah, baby, yeah, baby, lay some on me. Spread some of that silver sunshine around and be happy."

Your talent is avoiding work by letting VA doctors poke you full of experimental drugs. You justify the drugs and what they might be doing to your nervous system and kidneys with a vague sense of patriotism, country and maybe a little God sprinkled in with all the other star-spangled bullshit. Somewhere a flag is being raised in your honor. Somewhere there is a vet getting the same drugs as you only he can't leave at night because he is bona fide crazy and can't even remember his name. You are full of great things, that is why they pay you. You are part of the control group—the normal. They want to know what you think, how the drugs make you feel. And for this they pay you.

"Hey, buddy," the Suit next to you says. "Bottom line is I want to know what the hell you're doing in here."

He laughs. His face looks like a split potato. You say "huh" and drop your jaw at him, hoping he will leave you alone. But there is no such luck. Angel has already hit him up for a Black Label and he wants to talk—a return on his investment, only he doesn't want it from Angel. He wants it from you because you have a pleasant face and look like a guy who might know everything there is to know about the AFC, the quarterback situation in New York, baseball, possibly even the weather. Your reflection in a Budweiser Beer mirror (the one with the horses and cart) confirms this suspicion that you are an average Joe. The world is full of people like you. People pass you on the street and they think nothing of you. That is what it means to be alive.

"I am normal," you tell the mirror. "I am the Great Maintainer," you say.

Suit looks at you like maybe he's picked the wrong pony and you are crazy. After all there are the drugs.

"Me," he says. "I've had it up to here."

He points to a spot just below his eyes, you've seen bullet holes in the same place. His hands shake.

"That's why I'm here. Fuck the job. Wife . . ." He waves a hand.

You nod, say "huh" again, and pray for loud music.

Suit looks at you like you are stoned, which you are, but not on any drugs he can pronounce or get his hands on.

"No comprende," you say. You hope this will scare him away, make him think you're rude or retarded or both. But he is a businessman—used to pushing. It is what type A's do, they push type B's, C's and D's around to get their money. Type A's don't go away. You know this because you have spent your life avoiding them.

"Don't bullshit a bullshitter," the Suit says, giving you one of those "I could love you or beat you" slaps on the back. At this moment you would prefer the latter. Your theory on life is that the world is full of people who need and deserve a random beating. You do bad things, fuck people over, maybe one day you get a knock at the door and it's a man in a black suit. He asks your name and when you tell him he nods and lays some wood upside your head. And when you are down on the floor holding your smashed face, you ask him why.

"Think about it," is all he says, and walks away. You never see him again. Maybe you put two and two together, learn that for every action there is a reaction. Consequences. But this is not for everybody. The world is also full of people who beat themselves up (drink, drugs, sex, sports, money) until they learn or don't learn.

Angel starts clicking his tongue, leering at this skinny-looking junkie chick shooting nine ball with a crooked stick. Angel has low standards, everybody in the bar knows this. His standards are lower than yours. His standards are two legs and a pulse.

The junkie looks young, pretty maybe a long time ago when she was twelve or thirteen. Now she is dirty and drunk and in this bar. Her hair is a mess and she laughs when she bends to take a shot because her ass gets grabbed by every guy in the poolroom.

A guy with a nose ring and black eye is making book in the corner on who takes her home first. She wants to bet on the bartender and pulls a twenty-dollar bill from her jeans and puts it in Nose Ring's face.

"Extra ten if I can combo the three ball into the nine, right corner pocket," she says.

Nose Ring sees her the ten-spot, says he has to think on the first bet, afterall there are barroom ethics to be weighed.

Joe Mexico, a has-been waiter and vicious drunk, voices his disapproval from the pinball machine. He is the only other person you know besides Angel, although you suspect the Suit to your left, the one with a face like a split potato, wants like hell to be your friend.

"She can't fucking do that," Joe Mexico says.

You watch as Nose Ring explains to the junkie how she can't bet on herself. From where you stand they could be husband and wife, fighting, working it out.

Two shifty-looking skate punks—too young to drink or shave—saddle up and cop a feel as she bends across the table. She laughs. You mark this down as her random beating: People who can laugh are exempt from random beatings.

Angel is not. He has been to prison, had his cock pierced (Ampallang—horizontal bar), lost job after job due to his drug abuse and still he deserves to be beaten on a regular basis. The problem is: Who to do the beating? After all Angel is strong, he has no teeth and nothing to lose.

You order another drink. The Suit next to you pays for it, mutters something in Spanish, laughs, slaps you on the back and stiffs the bartender a tip. The bartender licks his coke-chapped lips, touches his crotch and pulls at his nose. He's looking at his tip jar thinking about all the blow it will buy him. You figure him for semiannual beatings because he's under the impression that he's too good for this place and handsome.

The Suit slaps you on the back again and shakes until your head hurts.

"Cat got your tongue?" he asks. "I asked you a question, bought you a drink."

"I forgot the question," you say. And this is true.

"Why are you here?" the Suit asks.

You tell him that you couldn't think of anyplace better.

He nods.

"I've seen worse places," he says. "I don't hear any gunshots. Where are the whores?"

"I'd like to see worse," you say.

"That can be arranged," he says. "Anything can be arranged, my friend."

Angel leans into you, points at the junkie and says, "Hey, baby, hey, baby." Whistles some more.

In the poolroom all bets are off. Joe Mexico stands at the end of the bar, swaybacked, muttering to himself. While somebody pumps money into the jukebox and punches up Metallica—the perfect soundtrack for a day like this.

The girl in the poolroom runs the table on one of the skate punks, who can't keep his eyes off of her ass. The Suit buys Angel another beer to shut him up.

This is a bad thing, you tell yourself. Angel never stops wanting. He is a black hole of need.

Angel grabs his beer from the bartender and hops off his stool and stands between you and the Suit. Angel has b.o. and breath that could peel paint. The beer goes down in three swallows.

Angel asks you, "How about another? You going to pony up for the Angel? Be his friend?"

You tell him to fuck off and he keeps smiling, tells you, "I want another."

The Suit next to you laughs and drums his fingernails

on the bar. You smell a fight form in the air. In your opinion, which at the moment is polluted by the drugs they ran into your veins, the Suit is a stand-up guy—a real ball-breaker. You look to the bartender for help, but he turns and sticks his hands in the ice bin. Just then you have a vision of beer glasses flying, blood on the tile (Angel's, possibly even yours, but not the Suit's, people like him grow old and die in oak-paneled rooms surrounded by miserable family members). The music hurts your head. Angel leans into your face and smiles. He mouths the word "beer" and puts his hands all over the Suit, who you realize is drunk and ready for anything. The Suit slaps Angel's hands away and puffs out his chest. A real bad-ass motherfucker stuffed into a rumpled three-piece and pumped full of drink. You figure him for an ex-linebacker, some Division III school maybe—crazy, loved to hit, but had brains and people liked him, so he got sent off to an MBA program or maybe worked and hustled his way into the money. You, on the other hand, don't work. Instead you allow nurses to thread needles into your arm, drip drugs through IVs and ask questions.

In the hospital this morning they asked you questions.

Nurse: "Do you feel sad, blue, depressed?"

You: "No."

"Do parts of your body feel abnormally large?" The IV dripped three drops of some clear liquid that looked like tears. The room had no clock, you measured time by the drip.

"Well, no."

"Does the radio sometimes play your thoughts?"

You paused. Nurses love pauses.

"No."

"Have you ever felt like hurting yourself or others?"

You answered no, no, no, no. No a thousand times. You want radios to play your thoughts. You don't consider yourself a violent person. You do, however, have violent thoughts and theories that you sometimes let slip to the nurses while you are under the influence of whatever they happen to be pumping into your arm. They tell you that you are the most colorful member of the control group and after a while they learn to laugh at your theories and call them charming, followed by more questions about the room and your body. They want to know if people are out to get you. Your answer: No. A big long hallway of noes and then the drugs, more than you could handle—like a love letter straight to your heart.

The Suit says, "No. No. No. Not this time!" He is talking to Angel, who is panting like a dog. The girl has gone back to the poolroom. Nose Ring is playing cribbage with one of the skate punks, who doesn't understand why you need pegs and a board to play cards.

Angel stands and screams, "I want. I want. I want. I want." Nobody listens even though it sounds like poetry.

You have another vision and decide to stand just as the Suit swings a beer mug at Angel's head. The mug explodes, spattering sour beer on your face. Angel falls on the tile. His head takes a satisfying bounce off a barstool before thudding on the floor. The Suit stands frozen in mid-swing, a broken mug handle in his palm. You poke your tongue out like a parrot and lick at the sour beer on your face. You taste blood (not yours) and figure that it is probably not a good idea to be licking Angel's blood, or anybody's blood for that matter. You look at the Suit and see a failed psycho linebacker with gray hair and a face laced with gin blossoms.

"Worse," you say, but nobody hears you.

The bartender screams something and hops up on the bar, crouches into a karate stance. He moves his hands like Chinese fans and snarls at the Suit. The poolroom crowd huddles in the archway carrying cue sticks for weapons. One of the skate punks has his chain-wallet circling over his head ready to strike. You point at the Suit, who drops the mug handle to the floor and wraps his arms around you. Angel lies between you as you try hard to conjure up some sympathy for him, but the urge to send him a kick circles around your brain like a buzzard.

The Suit begins to sob into your chest.

"I dunno what happened," he says. "I mean one minute . . . There's going to be hell to pay for this."

Just then the bartender lets fly with a roundhouse kick followed by a series of chops. Everything misses and he snarls some more. You give him points for an impressive crouch and menacing snarls and wonder what kind of Bruce Lee shit he'd be kicking ass with if it wasn't for the blow and late hours.

You resist any comforting words you might whisper into the Suit's ear. Angel groans underneath your feet as the cut in his skull rivers blood out onto the tile. The blood makes sucking sounds when you try to move your feet. You tell yourself that it could be worse, and you try to imagine how. There will be police and questions. Answering no will not be an option this time. The Suit will claim you as a friend, maybe even his best buddy. The drugs will pass out of your system nd the world will seem normal and controlled again. You will have to state your full name and occupation for the record—Carpenter/Guinea Pig.

Then you hear Nose Ring taking bets on whose ass the mug-swinging Willy Loman will take on next. Your name is mentioned—people always hurt the ones they love.

The Suit's clench tightens into a bearhug.

"You understand," he says, sobbing, and it's like he's coming apart on you. Air becomes a priority. Through the buzz of the bar you hear Joe Mexico taking action on your ass going down hard. You shuffle out of Angel's blood, which is more than a pool. A lake.

"What do I understand?" you ask, trying to push away from the Suit's embrace.

But he goes clamp happy on you. Things crack in your chest. Air is like cement in your mouth. Together you slip on Angel's blood. The Suit whispers sweet nothings into your ear. Odds are this is where your random beating theory queers. You let them pump drugs into you, poke at your brain with stupid questions. You work jobs that you hate because they beat you up. And now this? There is good money out there and even odds that you're going down next. And you want what? You understand?

ACKNOWLEDGMENTS

Thanks to: Gordon Kato. Bill Thomas. Eileen Pollack. Alyson Hagy. Charlie Baxter. Nick Delbanco. Keith Taylor. Ilena Silverman. Andrea Beauchamp. Lee Smith. Nan Graham. Carol Houck Smith. Susannah Meadows. Deborah Cowell. Leah Stewart. Adrienne Miller. Howie Sanders. Richard Green. Brad Jenkel. Mike Deluca. Jay Stern. Allison Cherwin. Megan Bradley. Tom and Charlotte Reid. Phil and Karen Moore.